Caught in an Avalanche

Caught in an Avalanche

Pankaj Kumar

PARTRIDGE
A Penguin Random House Company

ISBN: Hardcover   978-1-4828-4187-9
             Softcover   978-1-4828-4188-6
             eBook   978-1-4828-4186-2

To order additional copies of this book, contact
Partridge India
000 800 10062 62
orders.india@partridgepublishing.com

www.partridgepublishing.com/india

Dedicated in the memory
of my grandfather
Shree Mahabir Prasad Srivastava
who taught me the first letters of English alphabet

Acknowledgements

My sincere thanks are due to:–

My daughter Pranjala for assisting me to get this book published.

Nidhi Tewari and Alka Kumar for editing & proofreading the manuscript.

Angeline Bates for untiringly persuading me.

The entire team of Partridge India.

BOOK ONE

The moon was shining brightly as I entered the village of Bidar. Oh, the Moon! Ever so overrated! Is it only because of being one of its kind? Nevertheless it is the most enchanting sight accessible to every eye at the lift of a chin and sometimes even without that. It has been a permanent companion in times of pleasure and distress to enumerable species living on earth, through the years. The moon was however not the object of my admiration that night. I stood atop a small mound like a conqueror and surveyed the valley. The chill was pleasing. It entered the pours just short of giving a shiver. Huge mountains stood facing me reminding me of the challenges ahead. Yet tonight they stood majestic and calm under the moon. Oh! The moon again. I could feel the friendliness in the valley. The mountain rivulets flowed hurriedly towards their destination. The noise produced while rushing down was music to the ears. The houses and their unknown occupants inside were all lost in slumber. Even the alleys and the winding pathways leading to remote houses slept soundly. Only a dog barked occasionally. Everything was covered under the blanket of moonlight. Peaceful and content, so unlike to what I had imagined before stepping foot on the soil of Bidar. Everything was woven together in charm and glow of the moon. Yes, the moon had played its part. Without the moon it would not be the way it was. We had come here with a purpose of curbing violence. At this point of time, I did not seem to fit in anywhere. It was no place for battle, soldiers or guns.

I slowly unbuckled my belt with the holster that contained a loaded pistol. My assistant soldier, who stood next to me, promptly took it away. His relief was much greater than mine. He had to ensure the safety of the weapon. He couldn't rest till it was securely locked in the armory. He waited for me to get into my room. A cool gush of air brushed me on my face. The cold breeze was sheer pleasure. I was romancing with nature. The confines of four walls were nowhere in my scheme of things at the present. "Please go and rest, I will take some time." I told him and waited for another surge of breeze. It obliged me very soon. In such pleasing company my thoughts went back to the place where I had just come from.

'You are not far away dear; I can feel you all around. Everything that I see and inhale, it's you my beloved.' I said to myself as I began to walk up the mountain road.

"Sir, where do I put my machine gun?" It was a jarring query, much out of context; in contrast to where I was in my thoughts. Far away in a different world; I was romancing.

'Put it through my heart,' I felt the urge to say. The heart is ever so obliging to make a sacrifice. It is the quality of the heart which is exploited by men in love. A soldier romances with his weapons. The machine gun was the most potent of the arsenal presently available and it was his duty to ensure that it was deployed to its best advantage. Rather than err on the matter he thought it wise to get my opinion on the deployment. It was also likely that he was trying to show his alert presence to me. I was sure; Rai would have told him where to put his weapon. Anyway, I guided him to the vantage point that covered the vulnerable areas of the camp and also the most likely approach any intruder would possibly take.

"Put it there," I said and continued my walk. Not a soul was to be seen or heard. There were some footsteps behind me. "Sir, should I come along?" It was my escort, with his AK47 flung across the shoulders. He had not realized that I would be venturing out at this unearthly hour. He had settled down for dinner with a relaxed frame of mind. Assuming I was now in safe territory and his services were not required.

"No, you don't have to come along, I am not going anywhere. And yes, tell everyone else to break off and settle for the night," I said, clarifying that there would be no further activity for the night except the routine. I continued with my little walk. He took a step back, and then waited, not a bit convinced with my decision. How could I venture out into unknown territory without him? He turned back slowly, apprehensive and hesitant with one ear waiting for an amendment to my order.

"Go back soldier," I commanded. He briskly turned and marched back to the barrack, leaving me to my fate.

I went a little ahead, negotiating a minor bend on the road. I would have barely taken a few steps when there was a thud. It wasn't loud but it was sudden. It gave me a shock that made my heart leap out. I felt cold ice and a slight wetness under me. I was on the ground on my backside, seated like a fool on the road. The thud was none other than that of my falling. The water on the roadside had frozen to form sleet. Even my military boots could not hold me from slipping on the glass like surface created by the ice. The shock changed into jest, I could afford to laugh at myself as long as no one shared the joke with me. I sat there for a moment pondering; the road ahead was not going to be easy.

It was the autumn of year 1995 in the valley of Kashmir, the ancient land of Saints and Sages. The situation in the valley had taken a turn. In 1989 after the Soviet withdrawal from Afghanistan, insurgency broke out in Kashmir. A great number of militants got disengaged from Afghanistan. The ISI combined this force with indigenous militants and put them in the valley with weapons and ammunition. The period up till 1994 was one of great turmoil. A large number of youth were brainwashed and sent across the line of control for training in militant activities. The Kashmiri Pundits were made to flee from their home land and abductions were aplenty. The security forces put an end to this mayhem with an iron hand and brought the situation somewhat under control. This forced the main indigenous militant group to announce a unilateral ceasefire. 1995 onwards, the militancy was restricted to the foreign militants of the Lashkar-e-Toiba, Harkat-ul-Mujahedin and Harkat-ul-Ansar with small indigenous groups working in collusion with them. The militants operated from high reaches of the mountains. They came down for replenishments and raids. These small terrorist cells were largely independent and difficult to track as the terrain afforded them an excellent cover. They were always on the move and had minimum logistics and communication requirements. They terrorized the locals and obtained favours from them. In May 1995 the destruction of the 15th century shrine, Charar-e-Sharief was the biggest incident of violence in that period perpetrated by Mast Gul, the terrorist who became a household name at that time. The infamous abduction of six foreign tourists from Pahalgam was terrorist's handy work. A Norwegian tourist was brutally beheaded by them. The fate of others was never clearly known.

These vicious acts of violence by the terrorists were to hog the limelight and give an impression to the outside world that the situation in the valley was out of control. Yet the situation was not so bad, the state of affairs were returning to normalcy, albeit slowly. The democratic process of elections was fast becoming a reality. The militants wanted to spread their wings beyond the valley to the regions of Rajouri, Doda and Kishtawar. The route to these regions was through Poonch. To supplement the diminishing militant force the ISI had decided to induct as many terrorists as were feasible. Their main aim now was to sabotage the political process in the state.

The terrorists always tried to sneak into the valley from across the border just before the fall of winter as during the winter, snow clad passes made their entry impossible. To counter the influx of terrorists, the Army had been tasked to extend vigil on all the passes. Most of these routes had never been operative earlier and needed no permanent deployment, except for some Border Security Force posts. My company had moved in the morning to cover these routes in the Bidar region. I was the last one to join them. Our task was to begin straightaway from the very next day.

I returned from my short and solitary walk earlier than I had intended. I did not want my escort chasing me again. There was an eerie silence inside the camp. Things were waiting to be done. Equipment and stores still in disarray, spread all over the place. Yet no job was more important than the well-deserved rest after a treacherous fourteen-hour drive. Security of the camp could however not be compromised at any cost. All other work could wait till the morning. I went around the camp for a check. Sentries were at their places, alert as ever, smiling and cheerful. It always gave a good feeling to see dedicated soldiers. Satisfied with the arrangements, I entered my small dwelling that would be my home for the next few months or so. A nice looking cot had been arranged for me from the village somewhere. There was even a bed side table and a makeshift cupboard. A glass of hot water was placed by the bed side. How thoughtful! I always had a glass of warm water before going to sleep. I quickly changed and tucked myself cozily in bed, surprisingly, I felt at home.

Life was so unpredictable and fast changing. Only the other day I was at Secunderabad driving past the Hussain Sagar. The day was never complete till we crossed the Tank bund road for a drive into Hyderabad, the city famous for biryani and the majestic Charminar. The place was full of life. I was winding up the Battalion's rear party when I was called up, and overnight, I did not even realize when I crossed the whole of central India, almost nonstop and reached the crown. 'It's your first independent assignment my boy,' the commanding officer had told me at Sunderbani. 'You move ahead, we will follow you.'

The morning sun normally does not wake me on its own. But that day it did. I moved out of the room. Ah! It was so different. The sun and the moon seemed to change half the world between them. All those things that spoke so sweetly under the milky moonlight had lost their familiarity and friendliness. It was a little disturbing. A sense of losing something very personal hit me momentarily. The loss was however soon recovered when I went into details. I couldn't deny the charm of the silhouetted beauty of everything around that slowly came into my vision. I inhaled the fragrance of morning freshness. The niceties of nature were magnificently visible in every creation that met my eye. I was overawed.

The machine gun planted at the vantage point last night to cover the approach that led to the campsite was pointing skywards.

"Bring it down you dumb soldier, the devil does not come here from the sky," I yelled at the new recruit. The shout sounded gruff to my own ears in the splendor of nature. Quietly I murmured an apology to the environs.

There was absolute stillness all around; even the trees did not sway. There was a pleasant breeze that caressed the cheeks but it did not move anything. The dew from the leaves was beginning to evaporate. Except for the disappearing water droplets nothing changed. Or so it seemed. I was not to know, about the life that thrived under those thatched and occasional tin roofs that spread in small clusters all along the slopes. They were a sight in themselves. Beautifully placed on available flat pieces of land all along the green slopes, they too seemed almost natural.

"There is a message sir." The runner had slowly come and stood behind me while I was lost in my thoughts. He breathed down my neck from behind, holding the message book.

"Please get me some tea first." Though tea was not such a requirement, I wanted to inhale as much beauty as I could before silly little things cluttered my mind.

"I thought you were still sleeping sir." The messenger appeared sorry for intruding in my routine but someone must have told him that the communication was important.

"Sleeping I was, you fool." I laughed off his embarrassment, "but not anymore, how could one be sleeping with so much to do." He nodded baring all his teeth foolishly at me. The unwise like to be called names but only by those who love their foolishness without prejudice. I took the message book from him while he rushed to arrange for a cup of tea.

'Jabbar Mullick would possibly be crossing over from Gazala tonight,' the message read. So, that was the urgency. We were already in business. I would have a word with the Adjutant, but before that I wanted to do my home work. I called for the map and all available details on Jabbar Mullick.

I poured over the map, toothbrush in hand not wanting to waste even a minute. I couldn't see the pass mentioned in the message, "Get me the grid reference of that place, will someone." I wanted to get over it quickly, that in any case was the appropriate way of finding a location on the map.

"It's so obvious that you won't miss it sir, that's what the Adjutant had said," informed someone from behind.

"But where is the grid reference?" I was losing my cool; after all it was my first day.

"He didn't give it, sir." was the diffident reply.

"What the hell! There is no Gazala for a hundred miles on this map," I threw the map in disgust and took to brushing my teeth.

"My toothpaste! Get me some more toothpaste please." The dryness of the brush without the toothpaste was irritating. I would never have asked anyone for a thing like that all my life but this was official. I made a pathetic sight in crushed pajamas, with uncombed hair and a toothbrush without the paste in hand, presiding over a meeting in the office.

"Here it is sir."

"Will you put it on the tooth brush for me, please?" I requested very politely, as I was already preoccupied with the process of getting ready to make up for the lost time.

"No sir, its Gazala I am talking about." The voice was louder this time; obviously Gazala was more important than the toothpaste. The man was energized.

"Where is it?" I sprang up from the bed, with only one shoe on, "Why didn't I see it earlier?"

"There sir," the intelligence NCO pointed to a spot on the map, wiping the remaining toothpaste off the map sheet. Surely it was there, right in the centre of the map, bold and clear.

After having spoken to the Adjutant and getting as much detail as he had, I worked out my plan quickly and passed the essential orders. Once again I sat down at my observation post, this time with a military mind. I was accessing the correctness of our camp site. The camp was on a high ground and there were no covered approaches to it. That was good for security of the camp. I continued to study the area for a detailed survey. As life began to erupt all around the camp, I realized that there was not just natural beauty alone that surrounded us. My binoculars particularly stopped at one of the many rooftops. She was separating maize from the stem. The binocular lingered longer than necessary at that place. I wondered if she had noticed the intrusion.

The day was scheduled to be very busy. Not what one likes on the very first day in office. Couldn't Jabbar wait for a few days? Doesn't one crave for a relaxed cup of strongly brewed coffee before opening the first file? That was of course wishful thinking. I had to get cracking. The three men I had called for were waiting outside the makeshift office that the boys had put up; I stepped in and asked them to follow. It was the reconnaissance patrol, I had chosen for a first hand information collecting mission. My advance party had been in the region for a few days, but most of us were new in the area. Before undertaking any mission it was important to get knowledge of the ground and the enemy. I could get very little information on Jabbar, but the ground was available to me for surveillance.

"Gazala top should be about an hour's walk once you cross the broken bridge on the Gazala nala next to this village," I pointed at the village on the map, "Dhanna, yes that's what this village is called, and keep a distance from the site. In no way should you give out your intentions." I cautioned Rai, the patrol leader. Rai headed my Intelligence section too. I wasn't sure of his intelligence, but I had absolutely no doubts about his instincts. Being the first time, I elaborated on even the minor points of the assignment and its execution. I admired their patience on hearing my fourth repetition with the same attentiveness. That was the quality of a true soldier.

I dispatched the reconnaissance party. Then I went about choosing my troops for the night mission; it was the first operation in the area, everything had to be meticulously planned and rehearsed. I mostly chose the experienced soldiers. Ambush was a game of patience. I studied the pattern of previous encounters, though there were not many in the region. I then waited anxiously for the reconnaissance party to return. They were taking a long time. Finally they came, loaded with information. I debriefed them and gathered all the facts and data brought by Rai and his party. I sat down in front of the map with Rai and carried out a detailed analysis of the terrain, approaches and the killing ground.

The Gazala pass is a beautiful saddle like stretch with high mountain peaks on either side. There are very few trees on the pass itself. A mountain rivulet originates from the left peak which is higher than the one on the right. As the watercourse descends, it bifurcates into two. One coming straight towards the Barari bridge and the other takes a circuitous right turn. As the streams head towards the village the undergrowth gradually increases. Which of the two waterways Jabbar was expected to take? It was most likely that he would follow the rivulet, I visualized. That would give him cover from fire and an easy way to maintain course towards his destination. He was experienced; he would definitely not take the apparent route. However, we could not afford to discard the obvious in our planning.

Even that had to be covered. I selected my ambush site after detailed consultation with Rai. The killing ground and the alternate killing ground were selected to give Jabbar almost no chance to get away. Having worked out my plan, I called in the ambush party for briefing. The briefing was detailed. I also planned an elaborate rehearsal so that the drills would sink in. Then the men broke off for rest. I asked Rai to ensure that everyone had adequate rest; it was also a very important aspect of an ambush.

The 9 mm browning would be of little use to me; I swapped it for an AK-47 for myself, checked the chamber and entered the charged magazine. I too needed to get my act together. Old soldiers have always preached about ambush being a fine art form, precise in everything. Its success depends mostly on detailed reconnaissance and preparation.

The whole day there was a buzz of excitement in the camp. After a long time the boys were to be out on real action. The younger lot were begging to be included, but I could not take a chance with the rookies on the first day itself. They would get their opportunity.

I did the final briefing to the selected party over a cup of tea in a very informal manner, just before we were to embark on the journey, "You are the STOP, Salim." I said to a very animated Salim Khan.

"Yes sir" he answered proudly, Stop was a very important man in the ambush party.

"What is your job?" I checked back to ensure the briefing had sunk in.

"No one gets past me, sir." He shouted at the top of his voice, just as my orderly, who was running up to me from some undisclosed location, passed him.

"Sir, sir," he was panting heavily.

"Has Rome fallen?" I enquired.

"No sir I have locked it," he said, showing me the keys of my room

"Then what is all this fuss about, dear soldier?"

"When should I give you tea in the morning, sir?" he asked me humbly, his routine chore, every night before retiring.

"I am having tea with Jabbar," I joked as I ordered the ambush party to march. He did not quite appreciate the joke. The slight hesitation in his salute gave me the state of his mind. I paced up with long steps to catch up with the scout and took my place behind him. "Six o'clock I will have tea, it should be real hot." I shouted from a distance. He thumped yet another salute and watched us disappear quietly into the night.

I asked the scout to turn right leaving the main road going into the village. Rai who was just behind me prompted, "It would be much shorter through the village, sir."

"There are no short-cuts to an ambush site." I shut him down, a bit astonished. I didn't expect this coming from Rai. Maybe the dust of inaction had settled on his mind. Perhaps it was his over enthusiasm, wanting to remind me that he had done a thorough job in the morning. A dog barked somewhere deep inside the village; it was just a routine bark. The sort of bark that the dogs undertake to keep their masters happy, 'the dog is earning his bone'.

There was nothing much to be done for the next one hour or so. The leading scout knew the route like the back of his hand. He had been here with the advance party. And then there was Rai to correct him if he wavered. My little snub earlier would keep him on his toes for a long time. His sincerity was unquestionable. However, this was safe territory; minor irritants dare not take a chance with us. I switched my thoughts to Secunderabad, besides the Hussain sagar there was Madhumita.

I had known Madhumita for a very long time. More accurately from the time she was a school going kid. But we were not friends. There was no need to be friends with every child your parents knew. Not until the day we found ourselves in the same hospital. My father was admitted after a serious bout of pneumonia. She had accompanied some relative to the doctor. There was a lot of free time at her hand. She spent most of it by my father's bed side. The next day when she came in to pick up the medical reports she made it a point to spend some time with him. Father was impressed and I was obliged.

We were at the location by eight. Very cautiously we took up our positions; I made a little amendment to the killing ground seeing the tree line and the undulating ground. I cocked my rifle, every one followed suit. Then the unending wait began.

The moon had not yet risen. We could not easily see the Gazala pass or the approaches leading up to us. If he had to make an attempt he would do it early before the moon rise. Jabbar knew the ground too well, he had grown up here. Only a couple of years back he had crossed over. While we had eight hours to stop him, he needed only fifteen minutes to get inside and lose himself in the thick jungle behind us. The dotted villages on the beautiful landscape that I had witnessed last night would hide him. It would be very difficult to get him out since we had still not developed a rapport with the locals.

My toes were beginning to feel numb. 'Keep moving them' I said to myself. It was approaching mid night. Rai looked at me with a question, I nodded my acceptance. Rai and two others tucked themselves under the raincoat and dozed off for a twenty minute nap. It was impossible to be at the peak of your alertness for long hours under the circumstances. Though no military manual ever taught this to a soldier, yet through personal experiences, a set of un written rules form the basis of various operations of war. Salim threw an envious glance towards them from a distance. I smiled at him. I knew he was waiting for this. He quickly took out his water bottle and took a big swig from it. That would see him through the night. He looked at me for another smile, I frowned. He quietly put the water bottle back in its place.

The night was passing very slowly. When you become conscious of the time it begins to pass even more slowly. I was concentrating very hard; I had to make up for the resting eyes. I glanced towards Rai, he was appearing from under his cover. We exchanged notes. Then I leaned on the tree and dozed off.

A little nap and I was fresh again. The chill had suddenly increased. It was the small hours of the morning, the most popular time for the terrorists to infiltrate. We were freezing, 'Keep moving your toes.' I said to myself, assuming everyone would listen.

It would be day break shortly. Jabbar did not oblige us. We shook our limbs and recoiled to our camp through the sleeping village. I chose the route deliberately, to tell the villagers that we were up and about doing our job while they slept. The village dogs barked. I did not grant the villagers enough intelligence to understand that we were returning from an ambush site.

Jabbar did not come that night. But he could come the next night. We had to maintain our vigil. The next night was longer than the first, or so it seemed as anxiety was eating into us. The night after that was even longer. All of us were always talking of Jabbar, so much so that we even dreamt of him.

The moon had not risen from behind the mountains. It was dark. We sat noiselessly with our cocked weapons; suddenly I felt something poking me on the right shoulder. I jerked it away. It poked again. And I jerked it again. He was pulling my coat. Now this was too much, I turned in anger. If it was not for his white teeth, Rai would be sporting a black eye the next day. He was nudging me to look to my right. I took the night vision device from him and spotted some movement behind the tall devdar trees.

The whole ambush party was alerted. Salim raised his AK-47 to his shoulders. I gave him a stern look, he brought the rifle down. How could he be so impatient? First time blues I thought. We waited with bated breath. There were four men. They avoided our killing ground. We divided our targets. Salim and Hari were to take the leader. That should be Jabbar. If he was taken the others couldn't get inside, at worst they would turn back and run. Rai was to take the second and Mani was nominated for the third. I was to take the tail ender. And of course Ranjeet would sweep the entire area cautiously but effectively with his machine gun. Illumination and grenades were also readied. My shot would trigger the fire assault. They were now about hundred meters from us. We waited; it was too far for a confirmed shot at night. They were not approaching us squarely. That would be asking for too much. The gap between us reduced very slowly. It was around seventy five meters now.

It was a dark night; if we missed the first shot they would not give us a second chance. The tree line was too close to them. Most of the machine gun fire would become ineffective once they had the cover of the trees. We had to take them in the very first blast. I could feel the sweat running down my temple. The decision was crucial. Sixty meters now. Should I or should I not? Jabbar could hear even a muscle twitch or smell the hair oil used by someone in the morning. I knew his type. Fifty meters now. God! This has been longer than a ten mile run. I gave a sideward glance. All ears were cocked on to me. Just forty meters.

I took a deep breath and felt Rai do the same. I looked through the back sight, aligning as best as I could, I moved my index finger. The trigger tightened. I pulled it. There was a big bang. Rai, Salim and myself had fired simultaneously. The others followed a fraction of a second later.

The three dropped dead, followed by the fourth. What is this! I held the 9 mm in my hand, still smoking. I never carried this one. I thought. No I was sure. What's gone wrong, something had.

"Sir, tea sir!" I heard my helper shouting almost into my ears.

I sprang up from my bed. "Where is Jabbar?" I demanded to know straightaway. It was sometime before I realized that it was a dream.

"He is not coming for now, sir," was the curt reply synchronized with the unusually loud noise that the mug of tea made as he kept it on the improvised table.

"What do you mean?" I still retained some of the sequences of my dream fresh in my memory.

"That's what the message says." He pushed the intelligence report in front of me, of which he could not read a word, yet knew precisely what the message meant.

'Jabbar has aborted his attempt to infiltrate due to the strict alertness of the troops. Instead he had gone in for training and recruitment as ordered by high command and won't attempt the crossing for some time now.' The intelligence report was fairly precise and elaborate.

Suddenly I felt unemployed. What was I to do if no one wanted to infiltrate? The mind has its own inertia;

occasionally it takes time to separate good from the evil. I allowed my mind to take its own time. To do that, I slipped back into the cozy sleeping bag. Sleep was not easy to come. The other way to occupy time was to join up with Madhumita, wherever she was.

She, from just an acquaintance, became a person who was to be reciprocated with friendliness, for that one act of genuine concern. I did not take this as a burden in anyway. One often finds a different person under the skin once the ice is broken. She was intelligent company to start with. A reasonably beautiful one at that.

"Sir should I get you some more tea?" That was a polite way of telling me to get the hell out of bed. I popped my head out of the sleeping bag and asked.

"What time is it?"

"9 O'clock, sir." I didn't tell him that he was joking. I always told my sister that. It was no time to sleep even if you were unemployed.

I moved to the view point. The girl was there, separating corn from the stem. I could have given her a helping hand now that I had nothing to do. Jabbar was off our engagement schedules. He had managed to survive, for the time being at least. This was a game of cat and mouse. How long will it last? Now I had to find out, who alerted him? Probably the one who informed us about his attempt. There was money in this game, information was sold for money. A dangerous game it was of course. Maybe he was now trying his hand at some other pass. Or there was no Jabbar at all. Or it could even be a false message to make us slow down. I took a mental note of my observations. I had to guard against complacency.

The Jabbar episode had in fact diverted our mind to a single track of launching into operation straightaway. However my first task was to gain the confidence of the people. A section of the people always have a different opinion than the others, however the important part is, that the majority does not hold an opinion at all. This majority has to be kept on your side to succeed in any insurgency, as a military commander it is as important a task as that with the gun.

I invited the elderly and respectable people of the village for a cup of tea. As the villagers approached the camp with apprehension, we received them with open arms. All important persons were introduced by the head man. Everyone then settled down for my talk. After a brief welcome speech I came to the point straight away, "There are some people amongst us who do not understand the importance of a sovereign independent state. They do not hesitate to bargain for the freedom of our country only for a paltry sum of money. This money is poison and such men are not worthy of pardon, either in this world or that of the Almighty." They all swore by me. It was too early for me to know the weight of their promises. Heavy tea of course followed the meeting. It was a small beginning, lot more was needed to be done. There were others whom I could not address so openly. Inconspicuous meetings with unobtrusive people were also arranged. Not much was forthcoming. It is not easy to break the ice so soon. I wanted to explore other avenues. Putting on my thinking cap I came out for a stroll on the streets of Bidar.

As I walked through the streets, all eyes stared at me. I was an alien to the surroundings, like an unusual creature, probably with wings and horns. In normal circumstances I would perhaps be embarrassed by such stares, here I enjoyed the attention. I was meant to be different. Yet I was nothing different from them. I knew this but they didn't. That would help me in my task. A few of the bystanders bowed and wished me courteously, while some just wished. From the looks that I received from them, I knew they were cursing me from within. It didn't bother me. I continued my stroll with a smile on my lips. I did pause to listen to people who had something to say. I did even stop to converse with those who had politeness in their speech. It wasn't a bad outing, being just the first day. By and by as my figure would be seen more often in public, more and more people would open up with their ideas and suggestions. I was convinced by my first day's efforts that whatever happens here is communicated to the other side no sooner than later. It doesn't take the entire population to do that, nor did it appear that they held such believes. But certainly it was apparent and the message was clear. We are a part of the whole but you are not part of us. We will swear by you but we will see what is to be done next. We will not in any way turn against our own blood, even if it has gone sour.

I chanced to even meet Jabbar's father, or he found an opportunity to meet me. I was delighted at the fact that he had faith in my impartiality and sense of justice and the courage to meet me. It gave me a reason to ponder. I did not initiate the topic, only he began cursing his son and his own fate. 'What a handsome fellow he would make, but he is dead for me, let him live where he is'. In a way he was pleading for his life. I was perplexed by his simple logic to such a complex situation. I began to wonder if the lives of these people meant anything to anyone. Each one of them was fighting a singular battle, for the safety and well being of his near and dear ones.

I had no solution to offer to anyone. The situation was too complex to be dealt in puny packets. I had to do a job which did not directly cater for their problems. My job was to safeguard the sovereignty of my country and defend the lives of our people. In doing my job I wanted to cause the least discomfort to our people. Jabbar's father was also one of them. Yet he was not convinced that I was there to protect him. Neither were most of them, especially those who lived in the valley.

When the British left the country, the people of Kashmir wanted to be independent. No one seriously objected to it, it was a choice given to them and they had full right to choose. But when they were attacked, they turned to India for help. It became absolutely clear that its geographical location, its small size and limited resources would never allow it to remain a stable free country. History has confirmed this fact in Afghanistan and to a certain extent even in Pakistan. The region is too important to be left to itself. The Maharaja at that time had no other option but to accede to the Republic of India. That should have been the end of the problem and beginning of a new chapter. But it was not to be. The then Indian Prime Minister did not want bloodshed in his backyard. He declared unilateral ceasefire and involved United Nations in the resolution of the dispute. The greed of the neighbours and selfishness of some of the locals complicated the matter. Those who could were taking advantage of an already complicated situation. Unfortunately, the likes of Jabbar were not one of them; he was probably the victim of the situation. Yet my whole fight was against him and those like him. Jabbar had surely embarked on his mission the day we first went to Gazala, but he was asked to retreat by someone. It wasn't his father. He wasn't even aware that Jabbar was on our hit list. He thought of us as people who had just arrived on the scene and were trying to get our bearings straight. I had to look for someone else.

A group of children were playing in a small field, merrily kicking around. I paused to enjoy their jest. There stood in one corner of the field a boy who seemed in variance to the others. He was not following the game, whatever it was. Instead he was watching me. I became inquisitive, continuously shifting my gaze between the boy and the game. He was unfazed. I studied him minutely. There was something about him that drew me closer to him. I gestured with my hand for him to come. Promptly he was by my side, as if he was just waiting for the signal.

"What is your name?" I asked him.

"Moinuddin," his confidence for one so young was remarkable.

"You are not playing?" I asked, rather bemused that a boy his age was not playing while all his equals were having so much fun.

"I don't play," he spoke with awesome clarity and precision.

"And why so?" his straight forward answer got me intrigued; he could have easily made an excuse of not being well.

"I can't waste my time in playing." It was another unexpected reply that got me really thinking. Was this boy some sort of a freak?

"Come let's talk." I said as I began to walk towards the camp. He came without a question or doubt on his face, walking briskly alongside matching my pace.

"What did you say your name was?" I asked him as soon as the shouts of the kids playing on the field became slightly muted.

"Moinuddin," he replied with the same alertness, not one bit upset at my forgetfulness.

"Where do you live?" We were approaching the camp by now; he stopped for a while, turned slightly and pointed his small fingers towards the very familiar roof. It was clearly visible from where we were, as it was a high ground.

"You couldn't be living there?" was my instant response. I had been so used to seeing the girl there all by herself that I had come to think of her as the lone occupant. If at all, may be with old parents who didn't venture on the roof. A boy his age should also be jumping around on the roof. I realized my conceited thought and muffled my response to the extent possible and continued with a more straightforward query, "Is it where that girl is sitting?"

"No, that is Rashida, my house is next to her house, with the green window." So her name was Rashida, for a moment I forgot that I was in conversation with the little boy. I began to weigh the name against the person that she was. It seemed most appropriate, rather so appropriate that I almost mocked myself for not guessing it on my own. Moinuddin's eyes were piercing, making me a little uncomfortable. His gaze was sharp and authoritative, I didn't really appreciate it.

"Who all are there in your house?" My tone was harsh and revengeful in response to his alert gaze.

"My father, mother and younger sister." Moinuddin was unruffled by my rude stance; his reply was crisp and prompt.

"What does your father do?" This time I took a middle path, my tone was firm but not harsh.

He took sometime replying to this one, his gaze shifted from my face to the ground. He moved the toe of his torn shoe forming little circles on the dusty ground. I watched him carefully. It seemed that he was not in full control of his thoughts, "He works." Finally he spoke with a slight hesitation.

"Where does he work?" I asked rather amused, with all the emphasis on 'where'. We had reached the camp by then and I seated myself on the chair placed outside my room while Moinuddin stood in front of me slightly lost, avoiding my direct gaze. His eyes were wandering, trying to search for something but he wasn't sure. I was gaining ascendency, surprisingly for the first time that afternoon. All along Moinuddin had stood up to me on his terms, unwavering to the extent that I had begun to feel ill at ease. "Where does he work?" I repeated my question firmly, a little insensitive this time, after a sufficient pause.

"Anywhere." He said vaguely. I could see his mind travelling in time from place to place, searching for an appropriate reply. I realized he had no definite answer. I was gaining in stature while he remained to his size. My mind was running ahead of myself. "Where exactly does he work?" My rudeness shocked me but I was not to loosen my grip on the situation.

"Anywhere, where ever he gets work. Mostly in neighboring town, sometimes in far off places and at times in the jungle." He moved his hands vaguely to justify his answer. But he was not very happy with his own reply. My military mind was beginning to smell a rat. I had picked up Moinuddin with no particular intent. A suspicion began to creep into me, could he possibly give me a lead to something substantial.

"In other words you don't know where he works." I wanted to put him in more discomfort. I succeeded in my design. He became quiet and a little upset, the hurt showed on his face. He couldn't explain his father's occupation or was it that he did not want to? I began to probe him further.

"What time does he go for work in the morning?" This would give me some more inputs.

"Very early in the morning," he didn't hesitate this time; I softened my attitude a little to give him some space.

"Is it always that he goes very early in the morning?"

"Yes, but sometimes he doesn't go," he was reasonably relaxed now; probably the questions had begun to look routine to him or he had got used to my style.

"Does he stay away from home during the nights?" I didn't make any special efforts, but my tone had become rather friendly, which comforted him all the more. It showed in his reply.

"Yes, sometimes, mother gets very scared when he doesn't come home at night."

"Why so?" There could be some history behind her scare.

"She says these are bad times." He said very innocently. I wondered what he understood by bad times. I was thoroughly enjoying it by now. There could possibly be something in it. A son at this age should know what his father does and why should he stay away at night in such bad times.

"What is this?" I suddenly changed the topic, pointing towards my pistol.

"That's a 9 mm Browning pistol," he said with some pride in his eyes.

"And that one?" I was startled at his precise reply, so went further with my probing, pointing towards the rifle.

"It's an AK 47 rifle" he was very prompt. I was startled, though it was a 7.62 SLR, his vocabulary of the armory was definitely astounding.

"Have you seen this anywhere before?" I couldn't just stop myself asking the next obvious question.

"Yes," he said. My mind was totally made up by now. My lips rounded up all by themselves to blow a long penetrating whistle right into his face. He may not have intended the pause, but I created it for him. A jackpot! He was quite relaxed and I was getting excited.

I drew him closer and almost whispered into his ears, "Where?"

"I have seen it with the police and now in your camp."

I wanted an answer from him that would suit my perception. That was not forthcoming. I stamped my foot in disgust and got up. I thought it was a clever answer from a tutored child; he couldn't be so smart to dodge me like that. In my mind I had already attributed a terrorist connection to his father. His routine was so suspect. Weapons would be common place in their house; the boy would often get to see things. I was trying to extract the truth and he was trying to outwit me.

It was this preconceived notion that turned my excitement into a sudden burst of anger. "Don't make a fool of me; answer precisely what I ask of you." I shouted to his utter surprise and shock.

He was struck with fear. No one expected this to happen, not even me. He moved a few steps away, for a moment I thought he would run. Instead he turned and looked at me; there was a curious expression on his face asking me, 'Did I say something wrong?' I realized he had never contemplated running. The treatment was humiliating and the pitch of my voice was very loud; he only wanted to distance himself to lessen the impact. In no time I became conscious of my reckless behavior. I was loud, abrasive and unfair. He had answered exactly what he was asked. I sat down, recomposed myself and tried to make amends to my behaviour.

"Will you eat something?" he was amused by the sudden change in my attitude and conduct. However a tinge of fear was still palpable in his demeanor. He shook his head, declining my offer. I wanted to bring him back at a comfortable level, but probably irreparable damage had already been done.

"Are you not hungry?" I tried to be as polite as was feasible under the circumstances. He kept quiet, his tiny feet once again started to fidget with the lose mud on the ground. I waited for an answer. It wasn't coming. I got up from my chair and moved away. I wanted to give him some physical space meanwhile I asked for something to be brought for the boy to eat. I then very casually returned to my seat to start all over again with a totally different approach.

"Come sit down." I pointed towards the stool lying next to me. He very slowly came and sat down. I allowed him to be comfortable.

"What I meant was," I picked up the thread of conversation from where it had broken, "Have you seen a weapon of similar sort with anyone in the village?" He shook his head after a considerable period of time, in a most unconvincing manner. I repeated my question very slowly to be sure.

"No," he said opening his tiny mouth just slightly. The voice barely managing to find place to squeeze past, that too without any conviction. It was hardly audible to me.

"Are you sure?" My question was spontaneous, that was a consequence of his wary response. He took a deep breath. His eyes fluttered for a while before settling down. They had become moist. He was a picture of innocence which touched my heart. I almost wanted him not to respond to my question, just remain a child that he was. As I watched him sitting quietly in conversation with himself, I wondered if I had the right to be so insensitive.

Rai sent in a plate of sweets, as I handed over the plate to Moinuddin, he took it without any hesitation. It pleased me immensely to see the child like glee on his face. The eyes were still moist but shining bright. I took his little hands into mine, God! they were cold yet generated sudden warmth in me. His hands were full of mud as expected of a child. I was contemplating what to do when he gently pulled his hands out of my palms and stood up from the stool.

"I will wash my hands." I couldn't help smiling, as he rushed off to wash his hands at the washbasin.

He resettled on the stool with renewed confidence. Very steadily he picked up the plate and offered me the sweets. I took a small piece; he watched me closely as I ate, and then started to eat himself. I left him alone, diverting my attention to other things. I wanted him to enjoy his well deserved sweets. It was enough for the day for the little boy. Rai came in to inform me about the night patrol we had planned. As he left, I heard Moinuddin say something; I thought he was asking permission to leave for home. I turned my attention to him.

"You want to know if I have seen a terrorist in the village." He said again, seeing me turn my full attention to him. His question seemed out of context to me. My mind had already moved away from the discussion. His precise query gave me a queer little jitter. I was back in the midst of my presumptions. Was he all along putting up a front? It was so precise that he looked like a mind reader to me. I left everything else and returned next to his seat.

"Yes, that's the reason we all are here. I have to find them. Have you seen one?" There was no point beating about the bush, my objective was in the open now.

"They killed my mother," he was looking straight into my eyes. The half finished sweet plate was kept to a side. He meant business and was taking me head on. 'What do you want to do about it?' He seemed to question me. I sat down on the chair with a thud, running out of imagination. He was not finished with me as yet. He was waiting for his turn. When I recovered after his assault, I said. "But I thought you live with your father and mother?"

"She is not my real mother, I only call her mother. My mother died when I was small." His voice was choking. The eyes became moist again, this time with more tears than before. I had not seen so much pain in the eyes of

32

one so young. It was indeed a very touching moment. I sat helplessly. His eyes fluttered again and again. The tears were caught in the eye lashes, they did not roll down. While he was telling about his mother in broken and halting syllables, intuitively I took his tiny hands into mine. I gently patted them for my part of the conversation and let him speak out his tragic story. "The terrorist had come that night and killed her." He fell silent, there was nothing else to add, it was so final. I put my hand on his head and blessed him.

"Go home," I said rising from my seat. He stood up looking at me. The moist eyes had dried up but a question had emerged instead, 'You believe me now, don't you?' I was in no position to answer, I just wanted him to be back with his friends, "Go and play." I gave instructions for his quick return to his home. He gave me a smile but was reluctant to go. The meeting was unfinished. As I put up a strict stance, hesitantly, he started to leave. He had not taken many outward steps when suddenly he turned towards me and asked, "What is your name?"

It was not that no one had ever asked me my name. Yes what was my name! Considerable things ran through my mind before I could collect my thoughts and give a reply to the little boy. He giggled, and then ran away, giving me enough to think and ponder. I got up and went to the vantage point to look towards the roof; there was no one to be seen. I did not expect to be lucky all the time.

I went into my room and picked up the letter that I had received from Madhumita. She was very ecstatic about her trip to Singapore. In the pursuance of politeness after the hospital incident, Madhumita became an often pronounced word in my vocabulary. I do not know how and when from a verb she became an adjective and then a proper noun in the grammar of my life. We were meeting so often that when it was parting time we knew we had to say something to each other. And I proposed. However I really did not know till now that I loved her. Distance makes the heart go fonder.

My intelligence gathering mission was only a partial success. I had put all my resources at work. It was a slow and painstaking process. The people at large were friendly on the face but not so sure behind your back. I was always at a loss to understand the reason for their arrogance. We had always been helpful to them. I mean the Indian State and the Indian Army. Yet they always thought the help was not enough. Probably they were detached from reality. They had not seen the helplessness of the masses living in the central states, the abject poverty of millions of their countrymen. The arrogance was mostly caused by the bluff of the notorious, and their double game. They called the Army that protected them as an occupational force and the terrorist who killed and raped their own as their friends and masters. It was Ironical. The whole process of my quest for information and knowledge had got me little except for one called Moinuddin. Not many days after the first encounter I was one day reminded of him again. I lay awake at night, Moinuddin's tiny pained face revolved around my eyes. He was unusual. I slept with his thoughts that night. And woke up to find the thoughts still lingering. My orderly stood quietly by my bedside with a cup of tea. Out of context I asked him to go and fetch Moinuddin for me.

"Go and get Moinuddin." I ordered as he kept the cup of tea on the bed side table. Without thought or deliberation he quickly turned to go and carry out the orders.

"Wait," I commanded, he stopped and stood waiting. "Who is Moinuddin?" I asked him.

"I don't know, sir." he replied very truthfully and honestly.

"Then how will you get him?" I was irritated by his truthfulness; he should have at least clarified.

"Sir I will ask Rai," it was that simple for them, he would go and tell Rai that Major Sahib is calling you. Rai would leave whatever he was doing, even if it was the most important thing and come running. I would then have to explain everything right from the start. Therefore the best thing was to call Rai right in the beginning. However this was a personal matter and difficult to understand, so I tried to handle it directly.

"How does he know?" I was probing him to alert his mind.

"He knows everything, sir." That was an assumption of course.

"No, I am afraid that is not true. Moinuddin is a small village boy hardly anyone will know him." I started to get him on track.

"Where will I find him, sir?" at last he understood what I was getting at and came to the point.

"I don't know." I smiled in jest, "Why not ask Rai?" He did not hesitate for a minute; it was simple for him now. He wouldn't have to apply his mind, he quickly turned to go.

"Wait, wait." I held him back, things would be back to square one, "Rai wouldn't know where to find him."

"Then I will find out from the Numberdar." He was using his brains and I liked it.

"Okay that may be possible. But wait." Moinuddin's tiny fingers pointing towards his house came into my vision, "I will tell you. He lives next to the......" I bit my lips. I was about to say something that was not known to anyone. What would he make of it? Quickly I stepped out of the room, went up and showed him Moinuddin's house that was partially visible from where we stood.

It did not take too long before Moinuddin stood in front of me, looking a bit skeptical. I wondered what must be going on in his mind. Probably he thought I wanted to ask him certain questions about the terrorist thing. It was only now that I noticed that he was so ill clad. The morning chill was piercing into his skin and he was shivering, biting his white lips.

"Are you feeling cold?" I asked him in a matter of fact way, it was so obvious that he was.

"No, it is not cold." He was quick to respond.

That was surprising; he didn't want to accept a simple fact. "Do you go to school?" I asked.

"No." He shook his head.

"Why?" I didn't expect any logical answer. What could be the reason for a ten year old not to go to school when a government school existed within a mile from his home.

"I have work to do." It was unexpected, however I should have known that something like this was coming.

"Work! Where do you work?" I asked.

"At my house and my uncle's shop." That's the reason most children don't study, it was a fact, only I didn't connect the reality to my surroundings. Often we don't do that. I didn't hold anything against him for not going to school. I wanted to know his feelings on going to school so I asked a common placed question.

"Don't you want to study?" He gave me a simple answer, which again I should have predicted. "If I go to school, who will do my work?"

"Is the work so important, can't anyone else work for your uncle?" I said with concern for him.

"It's not about my Uncle, it's about me." He gave me a sweet know all smile, which was to become a trade mark in due course of time. "If I don't work, I will have no food. I will remain hungry." That was a rather strong statement from a ten year old boy. Before I could raise my doubts, he elaborated further, "My mother gives me food because I work for her." It was not his age to understand this fact. If he had, it was indeed telling on him and the circumstances that he lived in. A step mother, obviously! He was ashamed of his hunger, rather guilty. 'Why should one feel so desperately hungry? If it was not for his hunger he would have been master of himself.' The language of his body

37

spoke about his desire to be master of himself and not a slave of his hunger. So he worked as hard and as much as he could. His Uncle was no uncle of his, only a neighbor who extracted work out of him worth every rupee that he paid him. He did not say much but it was not hard to understand what he wanted to say. He was a very expressive boy.

I did not have any clear thought as to why I had called for Moinuddin that morning. Yet I knew I had to call him. My first encounter had made a clear impression on me to be sure of that. Moinuddin stood feeling the chill deep inside without acknowledging that he felt cold. He stood hungry and overworked for his age, yet deeply proud within. And as he spread his characteristic 'know all' smile, I knew why I had called him. I felt honoured by his frankness and truthfulness. I was only a stranger to him, yet he talked to me from the bottom of his heart. It was indeed very pleasing. I asked him if he wanted to stay with us.

"And what work would I have to undertake?" He enquired with a straight face, wanting to know exactly what he was getting into. Whether it would be worthy of his stature or not. He was a tough customer; life had taught him that at this tender age. Yet he was immensely pleasing, it was a pleasure to bargain with him.

"You will have to go to school and do your home work." He brushed aside my statement with a wave of his tiny arm. He wanted to know what would be his precise work in the camp; schooling was like an inducement I was throwing at him as bait.

"You will have to eat breakfast, lunch and dinner with us and go and play with the other boys. And if you still have time you will sit with me and teach me Kashmiri language." That was hell of a lot of work, from the length of my breath that I took to pronounce it.

"I don't understand." That's all he could say, the confusion was apparent from the expression on his face. He was trying to add up what it amounted to. Very slowly he seemed to get the meaning of what I had said. I felt contended after making the offer even though it was all unplanned and impromptu. It had all come from within. Moinuddin was a ten year old, or so he said, though he looked much younger. Light eyed fair complexioned, slightly built, he had alacrity around him which went beyond his years. We concluded our session after I had briefed Rai about the undertaking. Moinuddin left, still not sure, but promised to get back as soon as he could after informing all concerned. I went up to the vantage point and looked in the direction of his house, no actually towards the roof. She sat there, separating corn from the stem. She was watching me, I felt, though she was facing the other way. It must have been my perception.

He got back by the afternoon, with the real meaning of my offer having sunk into him. He was enthusiastic. As he explained the sequence of events that took place since the time he left the camp it was apparent that his father had jumped at the offer. His step mother was annoyed, but the father over ruled her.

"I will go back at night." He announced. That was fair enough, I thought.

The process of getting him into school began. It would not be very long before the schools closed for winter vacation. I was keen that he should attend as much school as he could before the closure. Initially he stayed with me like a shadow from daybreak to dusk, hardly venturing out anywhere. I got him a book to start with and his lessons began. He was a keen learner. Slowly he became familiar with the ways of the camp. Everyone was entertained by his antics. He was a man in a child's frame. Ever smiling, obedient, loveable, he became a favorite with everyone. However a humble servant's attitude had imbibed itself in him. He always thought that he was there for doing work and not for what I had told him. He insisted in doing things for me and even others. Small acts of kindness touched him so much that he could not endure. I did not stop him from doing these little things, seeing the pleasure he derived out of working for others. Soon he would be away to school for better part of the day.

His mother had died when he was four years old. He sometimes spoke of the incident; he remembered a lot for his age, the scene was ingrained in his memory. His father was a casual labourer, in and out of job at regular intervals. He married very soon after the death of his first wife. Moinuddin became an orphan after the marriage. His step mother treated him like a domestic help. They were poor people, but poverty was not shared evenly in the house, even there he got the least. There was no love. Ragged clothes, cold and starvation were his companions. The little warmth that he got from us was beyond his imagination. Moinuddin in no time became part of my surroundings. My hectic schedule allowed me little time with him yet he became aware of all my needs and noticed such minute details about me, even I had not realized their existence.

Finally we got him to go to school. Moinuddin was very excited. He looked a perfect student with his new uniform and bag. Surprisingly I missed him while he was away at school. A routine was soon set for him. He would get ready at home and come to the camp. Have breakfast and go to the school. Return and have his meal and then sit with me or Rai to finish his homework. He avoided going for play, instead he would do all types of work at the camp during the remaining part of the day. At sunset he would leave for home after early dinner. He wanted to spend most of his time with me, which was not always possible. When I would sit surveying the area and the roof he would quietly come and stand by me. One day he requested me to have a view through the binoculars, "Can I also see?" I put the binoculars on his eyes. "Have a look." It took him a while to adjust to the vision. When things became clear, he let out a shriek in excitement, "That's my house!" It was almost as if he was seeing it after ages. The excitement was understandable; I let him focus on his house as long as he desired. "Can you see your room?" I asked after some time. "Yes I can almost touch it." He said without taking his eyes off the binoculars.

"You leave your house now." I was in a jovial mood, seeing his excitement I tried to tease him. "Most of the time you stay in the camp with us. Even at night you should sleep in the camp."

He immediately returned me the binoculars a little apologetically, probably thinking that excessive usage will spoil it. He continued to look towards his house even without the binoculars. He had heard me without understanding the underlying humor; his spirits were not the same. I couldn't understand the sudden change. I tried telling him that it was just a joke and he could use the binocular to see his house as long as he wanted. But he remained silent. It was something to do with his house, I could only guess. I felt guilty; however nothing could keep his spirit down for too long, soon he was running up and down the camp.

As days passed I wondered how long this arrangement of schooling would last. We were not to stay here permanently. I speculated about taking Moinuddin along with me once our task was over at this place. I considered this option more deliberately. A thought about my old parents crossed my mind. Moinuddin could stay with them, he would be such a help. His schooling would also continue.

I was sitting in my office one day, waiting for the delegation of villagers, who had sent me a petition the previous day. Rai informed me that they would be late. I picked up my diary to record the incidents of last two days when a photograph slipped and fell from the diary.

I picked it up, it was that of Madhumita. I looked at the photograph intently.

She was beautiful in her own way. Her's was a beauty that took some time to be appreciated. All her beauty did not lie in her face. Her eyes were not extraordinarily large nor her lashes long and sensuous. She did not have a dimple on her cheeks nor were her lips delicate and thin. The color of her skin was not very fair and hair not black and neither as long as Rapenzul. I always felt very comfortable in her company. Never would I be an object of envy nor was there a pressure of competition. We could sit and talk for hours and no one was ever offended by our togetherness. Her beauty lay in the syllables that she chose in her speech, the length of her neck that she strained to look beyond everyone and the maneuver of her pupil that could see the unseen. Her sense of proportion was really appreciable and her liveliness was extremely attractive. All this took time to take a shape in its entirety. The perception of beauty thus changed very gradually and took time to be recognized.

Though I spent considerable time in her company, yet I was never desperately looking for reasons to be at her side. We never exchanged coy glances in public nor did we buy gifts for each other. On her birthday, I was one of the last to wish her. The beauty was that she did not complain. One day when my sister asked me, "What do you think of Madhumita?" I was left wondering for an answer.

I knew for certain that we were not in love, if that is what she wanted to know. Later that day very hesitatingly I told Madhumita about the conversation with my sister, just to gauge her reaction. And it was astonishingly similar; she was quiet for a moment then said, "What the hell! How can people talk like that?" Well how could people talk like that, but people would be people! Though on the face of it we took the matter in the most non serious manner, the repercussion of that day's discussion were rather telling. We became conscious of the fact that we were spending extraordinary long periods of time together. Our meetings became less frequent and discussions less vociferous. We were thinking more and talking less. A slightest physical touch embarrassed us both. Life carried on, though a bit differently. No one noticed the change, except the two of us.

The delegation arrived for whom I had been waiting; there were men of all ages. The older men bowed in respect which I reciprocated. The younger ones followed them with stiff arrogance and a scowl on their faces. I first addressed the older men and then asked them why the younger lot looked so stiff.

"The reason for their unhappiness is discontent but we are not here to discuss that today." Said an elderly man named Gaffoor.

"But we will discuss that anyway." I said with a smile to put them at ease.

"We have come with a request; the bridge on the Gazala nala is broken since the last season. It is deteriorating by the day and has become dangerous. The administration says they have no money to repair the bridge." Gaffoor informed with folded hands.

"The administration says there are twenty one such bridges broken in its jurisdiction and a dozen not even crossable. When the money comes, which is a remote possibility, the ones that are totally damaged will be repaired first." A young man from behind added to Gaffoor's statement.

"The administration does not understand that one day this dangerous bridge will take someone's life." Another impatient young man spoke in a voice that was even louder than the previous speaker. I was shifting my gaze from one speaker to the other one by one, wondering if it was an orchestrated and planned assault.

"So what do you want from me?" I said at last, not sure what they expected from us.

"We want you to make that bridge for us." It was as simple as that. A 50 meter bridge made of iron and wood, snapped at many places due to incessant rains was to be put in place. It was not a herculean task, but it did require some heavy equipment and expertise. I had none. I do not know what capability they attributed to an Infantry company. Of course the Infantry has insurmountable spirit and courage. That alone does not build bridges.

"Yes I have seen that bridge, it is really dangerous. I will come with you and have a word with the Tehsildar." I knew they would not take the bait. The army as per them could do anything. They did not want to hear about our limitations, a 'no' clearly meant that we were being non cooperative. An excuse to curse us, especially for the young ones with long faces.

"The Tehsildar will do nothing." It was a chorus from the crowd.

"We will not ask him to do what he cannot do. He may not have funds but he definitely will have something that he can give us." I tried to be as convincing as I could be. I knew in my heart that it would be impossible to extract anything out of him.

"We can give it a try." That was Gaffoor's voice after a long time.

"We will go to him with a concrete plan. A plan with contributions from the people, the army and the administration. Something will definitely work out." I told the crowd, they were fairly impressed; the grudging murmur gave way to animated chatter.

"That sounds good." Gaffoor's voice was more authentic this time and he was not alone in the crowd, there were a number of voices that agreed with him. We decided to sit at a later time to discuss further details. I did not forget the glum faces of some of the men that had of course lighted up a little now. Encouraged with the positive response I ventured further to explore into their discontent. They were educated men with no jobs. Promises made but no fulfillment. I tried to drill into them that it was a universal story, while it was the responsibility of the state to look after its subjects, it was humanly impossible to give employment to everyone. "Sitting in your homes and cursing everyone will not bring jobs. Moving out and facing the hardships of the world would make it more probable." I told them. "Improve your skills and don't hesitate to do whatever you get, through hard work you can progress." I gave them examples of our great grand fathers who left as labourers to Mauritius and The Gulf, are big businessmen and politicians now. They nodded in consent but with little conviction. I realized that the people here had taken the promises of the politicians a bit too literally. That had resulted in very little appreciation for whatever the Government had actually done for them. They were out of touch with the reality of the rest of India.

The next day I managed to extract an assurance from the Formation Commander to send me a detachment of Army Engineers with some bridging material. The detachment would definitely not make the bridge operational but could assist in any repair work that was undertaken by the Tehsildar. Armed with the promise I approached the officer along with the Headman and Gaffor with our request. The Tehisildar was very courteous but unrelenting, "Major sahib you don't know these people, if I relent to their demands I will have a problem at hand. There is no money in the development fund. The politicians have their own priority list and engineering department their separate plans. Bidar does not fit in anywhere." Then I told him about the help that was coming from the Army and the contribution the people have promised to make if the administration is helpful. The Tehsildar was impressed but that was not enough to grant us our wish. We were at an impasse when a young man entered the room with a big salam to the Tehsildar. "Sit down Abdool," he said disinterestedly and continued to block all our efforts to get the bridge repaired. We departed with little hope as he promised to look into the matter.

The next day was overcast with thick black clouds and there was heavy possibility of a downpour. Nothing seemed to be going in the desired way even in our efforts to repair the bridge. The Tehsildar had not given a positive response till now. The promised Engineer detachment could not come due to some scheduling problem. The gigantic, snow clad peaks in the far distance were covered with dark heavy clouds; strong cold winds blew over them and into me, shaking me right up to the bones. The peaks seemed daunting and devoid of any warmth and hope. Huge tall trees swayed from one end to other, threatening to snap from the middle. But the fact that they didn't was a testimony of their strength. They had the nerve to withstand the challenge. They swayed in rhythm and changed the harrowing sound into music. Courage can do it all.

Heroism sits on the edge of fear, romance on the edge of melancholy and hope on the edge of despair. Loneliness is a catalyst that works any which way there is space. I could not be guided by fear, melancholy and despair. The ice stuck to my cheeks and melted while the wind lost its velocity. I was romancing with nature and my thoughts began to flow with the music of the swaying trees. They wandered far and wide following the contours of the hills; they went further, over the rivers and plains to her. She must be thinking of me. Why else am I so delighted at nature's fury? A gush of wind almost threw me off balance. My fingers ached with cold. I rejoiced at the painful stab.

There was someone else delighted too. Of the more than two dozen roof tops that were in my vision only one was inhabited. Like my thoughts, her long thick hair were flowing all over the roof. She stood still yet her feet danced with the wind. She was part of the fervor and fury of nature. It was a sight that enthralled me. For the first time, there were no corns and no one separating them.

The storm was finally over. It left its stains of wreckage, thankfully not too serious. We got into our act of setting things in order. The Engineering detachment arrived to our great relief. They had also brought along some bridging equipment with them. We began assessing the damage to the bridge. We were greatly appreciated for our efforts in trying to repair the bridge by the people. But not all were happy; the issue of the bridge was not completely resolved. It was difficult for us to explain that despite our best intentions we had our limitations. The problems people faced were caused by lack of good governance and proper administration. The army was not a substitute for providing governance; it had its own role and agenda.

In one of my moments of nothingness, I sat outside my room. Moinuddin sat next to me on the ground. He was playing with the pebbles, hitting one stone with the other. Suddenly he gave a shriek of joy as one pebble hit the one he was aiming at. He was clapping his hands to celebrate; it was something he had managed after a lot of unsuccessful attempts. I left all my thoughts and began to follow his little game. After every hit he would further his target and continue. As I watched him, a thought crossed my mind and I was tempted to ask, "What will you do when you grow up?"

"I will be a porter," he did not have to think even for a second for an answer. I was just beginning to understand the meaning of his aspiration when he added, "But not here, I will go to Poonch."

His thoughts could not cross the mental barrier; most of the people he knew were porters. He had done well to think so much beyond his village. Poonch was a Town at the foothills, rarely anyone from the hills ventured further than that.

"Why not here? I asked as he aimed at a stone that was impossible to hit.

"Because everyone will say I am good for nothing." He was conscious of a porter's reputation.

"Then why not become something else, you are now going to school." He was quiet; I studied his face, I was not sure what he was thinking. In the few days that he attended school he had proved to be a good learner. Probably he too had the same thoughts as me. How long will it last?

"Will you come with me?" I said it with a jerk to counter the uneasiness that I felt asking him this question.

His little mouth opened to take in the sound that I created. His eyes twinkled in rapid succession. He craned his neck and started to hit at the stone aimlessly, missing it by a mile each time. There was no answer and also a failed attempt to show that he had not heard my question.

I knew I would have to classify my statement, yet there was very little probability of a response. I told him about the nice school that was just close to our house where my parents lived. And the lovely plums that grew on the tree in the compound. He just kept hitting at the stones. I knew he would reply only if he felt like; there was no point in pressing for an answer. He began to collect his pebbles, it was time to go.

"Good night sir," he said without a smile, then as an afterthought he added, "I will let you know tomorrow." I was a bit surprised at his unusual demeanor. "God bless you." I said as he left a small cloud of dust for me.

Next day Moinuddin did not go to school, I came to know through one of the villagers who had been to the school in the morning. Neither did he come to the camp. I waited till the afternoon, then decided to send someone to find about his disposition. As an afterthought I decided to go myself. He was alone in his house, sitting quietly and gazing into blank space of the walls. He sprang up in surprise, seeing me at the door, "Sir." That's all he could say. His eyes were red and he looked in poor health.

"What happened, are you not well?" I asked getting into the room.

"No, I am okay." He said softly, still a bit bewildered due to my presence. Then turned his head to one side and stood like an offender. Quite clearly he was not speaking the truth. That was his offence. I sat down on the rickety chair lying in one corner of the room. He apologized as it creaked, then came and sat down on the floor close to me. Moinuddin's house occupied a large space but it was comparatively smaller then the surrounding houses. Most of the houses were made of concrete and had partial tin roofs but his house was made of mud and stones. I inspected the room with curiosity, it was reasonably big. The walls were thick and neatly done with mud. There was probably another room adjacent to this one, bigger in size. A lot of space was open and a semi covered kitchen was in one corner. The ceiling had logs of pine wood converted into beams and put close to one another. Over the beam there was a layer of dried pine leaves and a mesh made of bamboo to keep them in place. I was not sure if it had a waterproof cover under the thick mud too, as was done in most of the other houses. I wanted to ask Moinuddin if the roof leaked, but it would have been most inappropriate.

"You don't seem to be well?" I said checking his forehead. He was in no hurry to confirm my observation as I looked around for unusual signs in the room. The room had nothing much to tell me. It had a small wooden trunk in one corner and a number of neatly rolled up beddings lined up on one side. A string tied to the beam on the roof at one end and to a nail on the door frame had some clothes hanging on them. A two year old calendar with photograph of a mosque hung on the centre of the wall opposite the door. There were some other things kept on a shelf carved into the mud wall, but before I could concentrate on them I heard him speak.

"No, I am fine." He repeated with even lesser conviction.

"Something is wrong then?" I tried to review the situation looking directly into his face. His face was pale and eyes were silent, blankly looking either in the past or the future. Moinuddin always fell silent when he had no answers, but unlike other children his silence always spoke. I was developing the ability to read his silence. His blank eyes began to fill with expressions he could only feel but could not fully understand. He did not try to utter them either, that was Moinuddin, anything that he was not sure of, he did not express. I looked deep into his eyes; they were somewhat perplexed yet forming into an image that replicated the feelings of his heart. 'I want to come with you.' The reflection created an impression that lasted like a film on the surface of water and then disappeared with the ripple of the waves. 'But I don't want to leave this little world of mine.' The image formed again. 'There may be nothing left in it but it is my own. Every inch of this valley knows me more than myself. The steepest slopes hold my feet and lead me to where I want to go. The pine tree tells me stories that my mother must have said to me. I barely recollect the face of my mother, but everything around here has seen her. She still lives in them. These walls have seen her; they are witness of her love and care for me. They have seen me grow in her arms. The mud on the wall smells of her love. I have lost my childhood with her going away; all that is left is her fragrance that surrounds me all the time.' Moinuddin continued to sit silently as his eyes talked to me. I thought I understood his dilemma.

"You must rest," I told him as I rose to leave. He too got up despite my insistence. He escorted me outside reminding me to be careful of the beam at the door. I gave a smile. We both stood outside his door and laughed for no reason at all. A strong breeze gushed at us from nowhere. Her hair almost touched my face. Blood rushed out from all my pores. She stood there, just there, so close, I froze. The truth of her existence, her youthful beauty wrapped in simplicity and innocence swept me away. I should have known that she could be around, I was totally unprepared. She was too close and so real that I lost my wits. If I had anticipated her presence, maybe I would have behaved differently. I turned away abruptly distancing myself from her as if she was a volcano. I felt challenged by an unknown force. It was a close encounter; my mind cursed me for being unequal to the challenge.

"I am getting late," I told Moinuddin as I hastened up the slope to hide my awkwardness. He continued to follow me. I forgot that I had asked him to rest. I heard him call out to me, "I have decided to come with you." That's when I became conscious of my slip-up, I stopped and said, "No you go and rest."

He stood still, looking me straight in the face, and then repeated his words "I have decided to come with you." I was about to repeat myself when reality struck me.

"Yes, yes why not, of course." I chanted like a parrot while he just stood and gave a faint smile. There was so much heaviness in his words. His announcement should have given me immense pleasure but it only made me sad.

He had taken the decision with a heavy heart. "Now go and rest." I said and he straightaway obeyed my instructions. I stood and watched him as my mind examined each step that he took homewards. They were weighed down with the burden of his decision. I felt no enthusiasm at his decision. Did he surprise me with his pronouncement? I was not sure at all. I reached the camp and sent the nursing attendant to give medicines to Moinuddin.

Next day I had an unusual visitor, whom I did not recognize till he introduced himself with reference to our first meeting. Abdool said it was a courtesy call as he was visiting the village of his grandfather after a long time. He was a contractor whose grandfather had once lived in Bidar, one of his cousins still stayed in that house. There was talk about good times and bad times and then a polite offer of help if I needed any, just before leaving. I thanked him for the help which I did not ask for nor had any intention of doing so, till Moinuddin whispered in my ears, "He can make the bridge." I brushed aside the idea as frivolous. I realized that Abdool had left but he was not gone. He was talking to some of my men just outside. I was rather curious, when he came back, apologizing for wanting to take some more of my time.

"Sir, do you know anyone in the Border Roads here?" It was a very direct question with certainly some intent. I was hesitant to give a direct answer. I did not know where Abdool would lead me to. "I am not sure; I haven't been in touch with them, what is the matter?" I wanted to know the reason before he could get me into any sort of commitment.

"The Border Roads are into a lot of work in this region. A number of contractors are getting work through them. I wonder if I can get an introduction, you know how things work." He was pretty direct, and I liked that, but I didn't understand why he chose me for this. I did not even know him. May be it was an afterthought, or had he come all the way just for this. On the face of it, the request was very innocent and not very demanding. But in business, referrals were taken to be generally emanating for exchange of favours. That was the tricky part. Moreover I had no idea about the Border Roads functioning. Seeing my dilemma, he was quick to add, "It is okay sir, I just thought in case you knew one of the Army Officers there."

I had not thought of it from an individualistic point of view. That was always possible. The good thing about the army was that a request was always taken in positively and the first reaction was to honour a brother officer's word especially if it was for the good of the organization. But what good was Abdool's contract for anyone except himself.

"It's possible that I can put in a word to someone but then what are your credentials?" I said with a smile, not to make it look offensive. However I was quite within my rights in demanding to know what I was getting into, if at all.

"Sir, I will never let down someone who cares for my people so much. Actually my aim of coming to Bidar was to see the broken bridge. If I could in anyway be of help. Only I didn't want to say it till I have made a full assessment."

I was quite impressed with his words, if what he said was the truth. And it did turn out to be the truth. Abdool had a good reputation in the village. The bridge however was beyond Abdool's capability alone. I made an assessment of the situation with the Engineer Detachment Commander and came to a conclusion that a combined effort by all could possibly make it feasible. Abdool could provide what army wanted including heavy welding and people would volunteer to work for the cause. The very next day armed with our proposal we approached the Tehsildar. He was very apprehensive initially. Then he realized what we asked of him was well within his powers and not anything very substantial. He gave Abdool a casual maintenance contract which did not involve too many formalities or too much money.

Armed with the assurance of the civil administration, we immediately set about repairing the bridge to the best of our capability. Abdool put in more than his bit and the small Army detachment improvised with the obsolete, old bridging material that they had brought with them. Gaffoor collected some real good volunteers. It was a sight to watch the villagers at work. The task was done in just a little over a week. Meanwhile I managed to get a foothold for Abdool with the Border Roads through an acquaintance.

We were in Bidar for about a month but it seemed we had always been here. Everything had become so familiar and friendly. Our constant vigil had kept the area peaceful and calm. One day as I was returning from the Barari bridge post after a routine check, early in the morning I saw an unusual sight. In the pre dawn dim light at a distance from the road was a small figure of a boy moving around a tree. His gaze fixed on the ground. I slowly advanced towards the silhouette. Approaching near I found the form was that of Moinuddin. 'What was he doing here so early?' I stood and watched him from a distance. He was unaware of my presence. He moved step by step around the tree, an epitome of concentration, searching for something, moving the leaves with his feet. There was a hum on his lips, which I could not understand. But I could hear and feel the spurts of shiver in his song. It was cold I realized. A gush of breeze violently shook the branches and the leaves of the huge tree. The breeze entered the pours of my skin. The freshness was intoxicating. The whole valley seemed to bathe in the freshness. The mountains stood calm like always in all their majesty. I was mesmerized by the aroma and serenity of nature that surrounded the child. My mind and my soul were stirred by a sublime happiness. I could feel something that I had never felt before. I wished for that moment to freeze and become a life time. Suddenly he met my gaze. For a moment it seemed that both of us had been caught thieving.

"What are you doing here?" I tried to hide my embarrassment. He stood there like a statue. Unable to come to terms by my intrusion.

He looked awkwardly at me as I came closer, then extended his hand and opened his fist. Two small walnuts filled his tiny palm so well as if they were always made for it.

"Walnuts?" I said, in a manner that it appeared as if I was not sure what they were.

"Yes, walnuts," he said, giving me full credit for guessing it right. I smiled as I picked them from his palm.

"You like walnuts?" he asked.

"I love them." I replied. Though it wasn't really true, no one can possibly love walnuts. It's got rich value but the wood is always preferred.

"Just wait," he said as he took the two walnuts from my hand and cracked one of them with a tender blow of the stone. "Please eat." He offered them to me.

"No, you have them first." I insisted.

"I won't eat, it's for you," he pressed on. I took the two pieces of walnut from his hand and put them in my mouth.

"You won't eat them?" I enquired, feeling a little awkward eating alone.

"No." He answered without an iota of hesitation.

"Then why do you come here so early to pick them?" I was inquisitive. He was speculating what to say, I knew it would be something unusual. He gathered his thoughts and after a bit of contemplation said, "I sell them."

"You sell them?" I was rather loud but couldn't help expressing my amazement. The intensity of my vocal outburst frightened him, he became uncomfortable. 'Was it a crime to pick up these walnuts from the jungle and sell them; these trees didn't belong to anyone in particular. No one had ever stopped him before.' His eyes moved uneasily, they did not know where to focus. I thought for a while that he wanted to hide behind a tree. A sense of guilt filled me with a lump in my throat as I watched his discomfort. The little boy waited in uneasiness for his punishment. I felt humble and small to stand and look down on him. I knelt and touched his cold hands. He shivered at the warmth of my touch. I held them with all the compassion that I could muster. My touch gave him comfort. He had probably not anticipated it; the warmth began to appear in his melting eyes and plausibly his heart too. He was unfamiliar to such show of kindness. His moist eyes could not hide the gratitude.

But like always he could not understand the meaning of my kindness or more rightly the reason for it. What reason would anyone need to show compassion to the god's most adorable creation in all its innocence? 'Poor child he was, unaware of the power of his childhood.' We walked back in silence; so much was said without words that we could not speak. A secret desire of possession filled my heart. The shivers that he had felt standing under the walnut tree and the freezing hands that I held for so long gave me a chill. The chilliness was an acknowledgement of apathy. I noticed, surprisingly for the first time that Moinuddin was grossly ill equipped to deal with severe winters. On return to the camp I ordered for warm clothing for him. It gave me some satisfaction to amend the mistake.

I then sat down to write to Madhumita. When the heart is warm, the thoughts flow very far. The last few months before we parted and I came to the valley, were a unique experience in our relationship. For the first time in my life I was experiencing a woman in her entirety. It amazed me to know, how little I knew of them. Knowing your mother, sister or to that extent a friend like Madhumita, as she was for so many months, was not enough to know a woman. Our friendship after that day's incident had come to a state of uncertainty. We were not sure which way we were heading. One day, I said to myself that enough was enough. I went to her and with no preamble, looked straight into her eyes and said, "Are you sure we are sitting here to discuss why Bill Gates bought Leonardo da Vinci's Codex Leicester at the Christie's auction for 30 million last month or would we still be here if he had shown no interest in the 500 year old scientific notebook." She was stunned for a moment as I continued to look deep into her eyes for an answer. Then she burst into a fit of laughter. Something that I had never witnessed before. The laughter came from so much within that it sounded like music flowing out of a flower filled with nectar and fragrance. Could I help not joining in? It was a new phase in our relationship. A chapter that gave me immense pleasure. This finally culminated in the announcement of our engagement. The engagement, however could not take place because of Madhumita's uncle's sudden demise. Then I moved out unexpectedly, in the call of duty. I did not write to her as often as I should have under the situation. She deserved more of my indulgence and time. Her personal tragedy, postponed engagement and my sudden departure were all distressing.

But I ensured whenever I did write, it was an encyclopedia of information, observation and emotions.

I had almost reached the end of my letter writing when there was a knock at the door. Moinuddin came in and gave me a perfect soldier like salute. He was dressed in warm clothing which my men had already procured for him as per my orders. He was overflowing with happiness at his new possession. My joy was greater. After the admiration he stood close to me with hands in pocket, unable to make up his mind about something. Then very hesitantly he pulled out his hands. Between his fingers were two soiled notes which he extended towards me as he looked into my eyes and mumbled something which was inaudible.

"What is this?" I said, surprised.

"I have been collecting money to buy kaftans for myself, now I won't need to collect any more money." He didn't elaborate beyond that for some time, so I thought he had finished. He kept his hands extended towards me with his eyes fixed on the ground. I was about to brush him aside with a cynical remark calling him stupid. Children should not bother about money! Then I realized he was trying to tell me something very softly, "It's a very costly dress, I couldn't have bought it even after collecting money for many months." My cynicism was timely punctured by his innocence. The seriousness of his speech was so profound that I put the unfinished letter to a side. I was now rather taking pleasure in listening to his monologue which he delivered with a childlike imperfection. "It's very little." He said apologetically. I looked at him wide eyed. I could not dare to call him stupid. I gently closed his fists with the money in it and pointed towards his pocket, asking him to keep the money back. If I was certain that I was not going to take the money, he was equally sure that he had to give it to me. His resolve was unflinching. I lifted his chin very gently and looked straight into his eyes to dissuade him; he looked back with astounding conviction. "Why shouldn't I pay for my things?" he said and I had no answer. He anchored himself with a slight tilt to one side and did not exactly give me a broad smile. But the sound of his resolve was quite clear. 'I am not as poor as you think. Don't be so generous to make me feel helpless and orphaned'. I saw the child who had outgrown himself. The child did not understand the compassion that I felt and the man did not appreciate unwanted generosity. In his little world he had always known that everything requires to be paid for. His mother gave him food because he worked in the house. His father did things for him because he worked in the shop and got some money for the house. How could anyone give anything just for nothing?

I lost the debate; he won convincingly with his imperfect arguments. My hesitant hands took the two soiled notes from him. "No dear, your collections are valuable beyond description, much more than a few pieces of clothing will ever cost." He did not ask me for any justification on my statement, though he appeared to question my mathematics. He just watched me as I gazed at them. "They are soiled." He said, I could not speak as a lump formed in my throat. I avoided his gaze to not give away my feelings.

I took my pen and wrote on it, 'My life's treasure' and put them in the inner cover of my diary. The observant Moinuddin asked, "Why don't you keep them in your purse?"

"I don't want to lose my treasure by mistake." I replied but he did not quite understand.

The trees were beginning to shed their leaves. Far in the distant clouds, the mountain peaks had lost their color further and the morning breeze brought with it the icy chill from those snow clad peaks.

"Will it get any colder?" I asked the porter chopping the wood who had paused to rub his hands. Moinuddin began to laugh.

"This is not cold." He announced, shivering a little even with the new kaftan. Moinuddin had slowly opened up and become quite talkative. No one could talk about the place in his presence. He was all knowledgeable. "The real winter will only begin after a month; we will all freeze if we stand like this for too long." He laughed.

"Then what do you do not to get frozen?"

"We stay in our houses with kangadi and blankets." He made such a gesture with his hands that I began to laugh. He continued giving me insight into the past, "Last year I didn't have my own blanket, but this year I have already bought one." I stopped laughing. I always thought parents tucked their children in beds. But I had come to learn that Moinuddin was different, still I was bowled over.

"You bought a blanket for yourself?" I couldn't actually believe it.

"Mother always scolded me when I asked for an extra blanket; she would always give me a torn one which would not hold the cold. So I collected and sold walnuts to buy a blanket this time. Now I do not have to ask her for it nor listen to her scolding on this account." He said with a smile. I knew the walnut story as also the meager resources that Moinuddin and his family had. He had very early in life learnt the importance of money. Money could change his world; it could buy him comforts, make his parents happy, stop his mother from beating him and reduce his helplessness. He was in a mood to talk today and as I showed keen interest in his personal life, it prompted him to declare his other possessions.

"I have also got a hen." He said with glitter in his eyes.

"A hen? Why a hen?" I was rather astonished, a hen was an unusual pet for a small boy.

"She lays an egg for me every day." He smiled his usual dimpled smile. "And I sell them to the shop keeper. Moinuddin was telling me how life can teach and make a child into an adult without using too many years.

I looked at him with admiration. Each day unfolded secrets of his life. He was a learner challenging life in his own way.

One day after school Moinuddin came to my office and stood quietly. I was engrossed in work and did not pay heed to him. When he was about to leave I realized his presence. I asked him to come over. He moved in and began to tidy up the office. I returned to my work.

"Will you be going to Poonch any time in the future?" He asked me softly not wanting to break my thoughts as I worked on a draft.

"No." I said almost without thought, still preoccupied. He made no more enquiries. I realized he had lost some of his enthusiasm because of my indifference. I quickly closed the file and faced him with full attention, "What is the matter?"

"I want to go to Poonch." He said politely.

"Why?" I was curious to know.

He was quiet for a moment, and then replied hesitantly, "I want to buy a gift."

That was a very nice gesture; I thought and began to laugh, "Is it for me?"

He became a little uncomfortable. Obviously it was not for me, but he was embarrassed.

"Never mind that, I am here to give gift to everyone and not take from them." I put him at ease. "What do you want to buy?" I changed the subject, since he didn't want to reveal his secret.

"I don't know." He said innocently, "It's for Rashida."

It was my turn to fall silent. The girl on the roof, she is his neighbor. I curtailed my curiosity of further investigation. What could be the occasion I wondered?

Moinuddin left the office without any concrete response from me. Our conversation had taken a different turn. I was unable to return to my work for quite some time. What could be the occasion, I continued to make wild guesses.

I called in for Moinuddin a little later as I had left his query unanswered, but he had left for home. I kept wondering what the occasion could be.

I was amused at my inquisitiveness. Why was I so keen to know such a routine little thing? Many times during the evening my curiosity would take me back to the same question.

In the morning it so appeared to me that I was eagerly waiting for Moinuddin to show up. I however did not make it apparent when he did.

"I will get whatever you want from Poonch." I told him.

"I do not know what to buy, can you help me?" He asked.

"You have to decide what to buy as per the occasion and the likes of the person." I tried to help, my emphasis was however on the occasion.

Moinuddin was silent for a while thinking what to say.

"I won't know what to buy till I see what is there to buy. I have never gone to a big market." That was a very valid point. I gave it a thought then conceded to his logic. But the question of occasion still remained unanswered.

I had come to know in these few days with Moinuddin that while he would tell a lot of things unasked for and even reply to questions not directed at him very promptly. When confronted with a direct question, he would always take his time and reply concisely to the point.

He was very happy that I had agreed to his request. His gratitude was in his eyes. The words were coming from the heart.

"Rashida is the only person who loves me." He said softly, "All the time giving me things that she thinks I need. I have never given her anything." Moinuddin looked up at me for my reaction. He was asking me if it was not his obligation to reciprocate. The child was speaking words of an adult. I was fascinated. Who would want anything more from him than he already gave? I thought it was true for Rashida too. She could not help loving him. Moinuddin was a bundle of joy. He was a marvel who stood like an apostle in the company of mortals. Truly speaking we were unequal to him.

Sunset is a beautiful sight, but is also a forlorn moment. The sun leaving the sky, parting after a day's sojourn and togetherness. Separation is the underlying emotion that gives a sense of losing warmth. The chill adds to the glum. The day's pains and pleasures condense and enter the heart. As I saw the setting sun vanishing behind the mountains, I wondered if I was up to the gloom that surrounded me. I had always stood up to loneliness with dignity and strength yet today I floundered. I looked for company in the thoughts of my beloved. What would she be doing at this hour? Reading my letter! Does she remember me all the time as I do? Somewhere within me I had this lingering thought about her emotional coefficient. She had always given me more joy than warmth.

I was sad and I knew not why. Loneliness was too dear a friend to give me despair, there was surely something more. A song emerged on my lips…. A song of sadness… that held me somewhat together in gloom and obscurity.

The haze was clearing for me to see what was in front of me. He was an extraordinary child. I was thrusting ordinariness on to him. The routine, the mundane and uncharacteristic would he encounter all his life and an eternal servant he would become. I would be the architect of his ruins. Would the real me not revolt against me. I was perplexed by my audacity.

The louder I sang the deeper it sank.

Moinuddin had promised to come with me, I was not sure if I wanted him to keep his promise. I knew my sadness lay in my audacity. I slept with my misery unresolved.

Through the clouds from the sky rode the magnificent white stallion. Flowing hair and majestic beauty. I saw it come like a dream in my dreams. On it sat a little prince, dwarfing the majesty of the stallion. His charm lighted the clouds. The silver clouds parted to give way to the angel. His smile showered petals of rose and his tiny eyes sparkled. An acme of perfection. I recognized the twinkle, the smile and the face. The magnificent sight left me spellbound. My happiness burst in the form of a shriek.

It was Moinuddin.

I sprang up to take the reins of the horse in my hand. But surely there was no horse and no reins. It was all a dream that I saw with my open eyes. A Prince he was; whom I let be a pauper. My impudence was infuriating me for keeping a Prince in rags. Something hit me in the stomach; it was a sense of remorse. The guilt that had always been with me but I failed to acknowledge. How I could disregard something that was eating into my consciousness? The guilt and the accompanying misery were my punishment. I honoured the verdict of the jury within me. It was a fair judgment, I was prepared to suffer. I slipped out of the comfort of my sleeping bag. The warmth was only pretence and no closer to reality than I was to myself.

I paced the cold deserted streets of Bidar in anguish. The moon mocked at me, 'Prince in the rags of a pauper, Moinuddin!' I had to take a decision before my bones froze in the cold. I feared the bones would become brittle and crack.

'Dear Madhumita' I wrote, 'are you willing to marry a father of a ten year old son?' I went on to explain the circumstances under which I was writing the letter. 'I think you will understand why I make this extraordinary demand of you.' I concluded. I was not sure if she ever would, but I felt genuinely good having written it. I could not sleep for a long time but not because I was incensed. I looked out of the window and saw the smiling moon. I could hardly feel the existence of my heart and of course there was no guilt.

The next day I went to Poonch and bought a gift for Rashida and gave it to Moinuddin. It was a pair of long blue stone earrings. I guessed it would go wonderfully well with her face that I captured in my memory during the close encounter.

The first snowfall of the season greeted us with aplomb. Those of us who had not seen a snow fall earlier were delighted beyond words. The sleet of white flakes descending from the sky, slowly at first and then in a rapid continuous flow was a sight to be savored. In front of our eyes the barren brown and black patches of the mountain side turned absolutely white. Gradually the whole landscape was bathed in whiteness just leaving the winding tarmac roads. They too would not be able to resist the cover for long. It was however only the first snow fall and all the snow from the lower reaches of the mountains and around the villages would disappear once the sun would come out in a day or so. The first snow was a reminder to the villagers to get started on their activities. Winter stocking of food grains and other essential commodities was the most essential part. Transportation after heavy snowfall would be almost impossible. Most of the men would also leave for places like Amritsar and Shimla to find work as there would be nothing to do in the village. It was also the marriage season. Those marriageable had to be married; nothing would be possible for the next five months. I was flooded with a spate of marriage invitations. I accepted some and turned down the others politely. Jalaluddin, the old Numberdar too had come with the invitation of his daughter's marriage. I had to find time for him. Although it was the most vulnerable time even for us and hectic activities of guarding the passes had to be undertaken. The marriages were a great festival of eating and extending courtesies. Jalaluddin had laid out extensive traditional kashmiri cuisine and he took pride in explaining the intricacy of their preparations. The yakhni prepared in curd was the most relishing. Even the way he described its preparation, was pretty exquisite.

It was also the peak time for infiltration. The terrorists had to maintain a certain level of activities throughout the winters to show their presence and nuisance value. While it was essential for them to infiltrate maximum men, arms and ammunition, the inclement weather also felicitated them. Visibility at this time would be so low that one would not be able to see beyond a few feet. The passes would have some snow but not enough to stop them. It would be impossible to infiltrate through the passes once they were closed after heavy snow. This was the time of our real test. All our preparations of collecting intelligence, cultivating informers and ground reconnaissance would be put to use. Our intention was to foil every attempt of the terrorists. Each day we would gather intelligence and resort to hectic patrolling activities at all the possible places of infiltration. There was no respite for us but no one was complaining. It was our job and we were here to do it. There was a sense of satisfaction and we looked forward to a fresh challenge each day.

I sat one morning planning such an operation. We had some specific information and accordingly we had planned to lay an ambush. As I sat with the map doing in-depth study, Moinuddin came in the most businesslike manner dressed in school uniform. He was rather early for school. It was quite normal for him to sometime come to the camp before going to school. I had very gradually tried to bring about a change in his attitude that was so deeply ingrained in him. My endeavor was to broaden his horizon and increase his knowledge base. With knowledge he could face the world with confidence. He came up to me rather hesitantly as I was engrossed in work and handed over a piece of paper to me. He retreated a few steps and stood close to the door, sort of waiting for a reply. "What is this?" I asked rather surprised as he had never done such a thing before.

"It's a letter." He said in the most indifferent manner that prompted me to open it immediately. For Moinuddin it appeared to be a silly question because it did look like a letter only, however I couldn't visualize why Moinuddin would resort to writing letters. I saw the letter, it was in Kashmiri.

"What is written in it?" I asked assuming he would know as I had hardly any knowledge of the language and my Urdu was also restricted to the basics.

"I don't know." He said with a slight brush of his hand. I did not grill him any further, I had just managed to read the name of the sender, it was from Rashida.

It was not just excitement alone that made me sit back on the chair and take a deep breath. My mind started running in many directions wondering what could it be. What had prompted her to write a letter to me? The possibilities were many yet I could think of none. I could take someone's help to read the letter yet my excitement did not permit me to do that. I sat up and began to figure out words one by one. The letters were so beautifully formed that the task did not seem impossible. It took time but I managed to structure broken sentences and envisaged the rest. It read something like this…

'Dear Sir,

I am Rashida, the girl on the roof as you know of me.' I took a deep breath, it was pretty direct, since when has she known this, I wondered. I should have been more discreet, well I could not undo what has already happened therefore I read on.

'My Sister is getting married.' So it was an invitation, I was rather amused, why should it come from her? Were there no elders in the house? They could have easily walked up to my office and extended the invitation like Jalaluddin did? Surely I was not convinced. I was taking time to shape words and read, while my mind was running ahead with speculation and conversing with myself. The next line took a long time to make some sense, it was rather confusing. 'I believe you are planning to kill my brother when he comes for the marriage. I beg for his life.'

I was astounded by the content of this small note, especially the last two lines. All the excitement and speculation generated initially evaporated into thin air.

'Who is her brother, why should I kill him?' I said to myself. How was I to get an answer? I looked at Moinuddin, may be he could give me a clue. He stood expressionless; he did not know my question. How would he, it was obvious he was not privy to the contents of the letter. So I repeated the question aloud for his benefit. "Why should I kill him?"

"Whom are you going to kill?"

"Her brother." I was not sure how much did Moinuddin know already and how to frame an appropriate question.

"She does not have a brother." That was his immediate response.

"Then who is coming for her sister's marriage?" I was astounded.

Moinuddin paused for a while, as if putting his thoughts together. "Is it Faisal you are talking about, yes I have heard about him, but he had gone away long back?" Faisal it must be, I thought and asked, "What is this story of Faisal?"

Moinuddin was getting late for school, yet I could not resist his completing the story.

"I have never seen him but I heard he had been picked up by the terrorists a long time ago at gun point. That was the time my mother was also killed. They said it was an accident." He could not continue further. I patted his back and saw him off to school.

I began to gather information; yes we had a lot of inputs. This was the time for infiltration, the terrorists would be trying their best and so would we. It would be difficult to say who would survive an ambush, but we had never thought of an ambush as trying to kill someone. It was a jarring thought. An ambush was a military operation, undertaken for a military purpose. I scanned through my files, hoping not to find Faisal's name in it. But he was there with a photograph fairly young and handsome, son of Sherkhan, resident of Bidar. He had crossed over to the other side in 1989. The file didn't say anything about having been picked up, as Moinuddin had suggested. But his age at the time of crossing suggested that it was quite likely, as no fifteen year old would go into an alien country on his free will. Later the file confirmed him to be a PTM (Pak Trained Militant) who was expected to be reasonably active this season.

I felt sad, of all the people Faisal had to be her brother. His name stood like a thorn from the file. I only wished it was a typing error. I came out of the room but was scared even to look towards her. I could see through the corner of my eye, she sat there motionless, not separating any corn from the stem. She just sat there waiting for an answer.

It was a question for which I had no answer. I was even amazed at the fact that she had asked me for this favour. Had she not put her brother's life at a greater risk by letting out his intentions? Did she not know that it was my call of duty to stop him from crossing over, and in the process he could lose his life. I was sure she had seen enough of the turmoil all around her to know all this. Yet she chose to make a request. She sat there, 'the girl on the roof' as I knew her to be. I saw her again, she was not just a girl on the roof, she was something much more.

I came in and sat down holding the small piece of paper in my hand and gazed at it. I could see her writing it. Why did she write it? I asked myself again and again. My dilemma had not yet sunk in, I was only thinking of the immediate response. Was she waiting for my response, what should I write to her? I picked up my pen many times and kept it back as it is. Moinuddin was also not around to help me out. I could only curse those who had created this situation. I looked up and said aloud to myself, 'Why do we have to do things that we do not want to do?' But we do have to do our duty.

I picked up the pen one final time and began to write.

'Dear Rashida,' I wrote and then paused, what language I should use. I was not sure if I could write a language that she would understand, but I had to continue, I used all the languages that I knew including words from them that I thought would be understood by common sense. I tried to match her hand writing as I wrote…..

'I must apologize for my language that I use. I am a soldier, and a soldier does not recognize a brother if he comes as a terrorist. His fate would kill him if he comes as one. But if he comes only as a brother and surrenders and vows to love and protect his country, I promise no harm would come to him.' It was easily written but I knew how difficult it would be. In what way she could influence him to do the impossible. My mind was unable to concentrate on anything other than the day's new development. I postponed the operation that I had planned to undertake that evening. At times I questioned my judgment. My heart told me Faisal was not a terrorist; he was made to be one. Whose only fault was that he was subjected to such a un-childlike upbringing at the behest of a neighbor, who was revenging a war he had lost because of his own doing, twenty years ago. I was upset with myself. There seemed no hope for Faisal. The thought was unnerving, 'What are we? I asked myself, 'and why are we what we are?' I knew my call for duty could shatter her life. I dreaded the thought. Would I never see her again? Seeing her every day had become such an essential part of Bidar that I could not imagine life without that. For a moment I was sad just for myself. What would be life without the girl on the roof top?

I had to wait for Moinuddin to return from school to send the letter to her. I read the letter many times before Moinuddin arrived to deliver it. He too had understood the gravity of the situation but was not fully aware of my dilemma. I sat anticipating the passage of letter from one hand to the other and the ensuing conversation. The reading of the letter would be such an onerous task. Would she read it silently or aloud? Was the letter readable, how well she was adapted to reading words that I had selected and formulated so deliberately? I waited for all that and much more to happen, then came out slowly on to the view point. The roof top was empty and so was my life for the time being.

"Tea Sir," The voice broke my thoughts as my orderly placed the evening cup of tea on the table. He watched me stare at the cup of tea as if he had made a mistake. The uneasiness remained till I told him to take it away. As he picked up the cup, I saw his eyes search for the fly inside the cup. Poor fellow! What else could be the reason for my refusal?

"Get me a drink." I said with such simplicity as if it was just a routine demand. The firmness in my voice however made him almost drop the cup back on the table.

"A drink sir?" He wanted to make sure if he had understood it correctly, though there was no ambiguity in my demand yet the intention may be otherwise.

"Yes get me a drink." I repeated in a very authentic manner. I needed something to fill the void that I was experiencing. The void was yawning in absence of a response to my obstinate reply.

I drowned my misery in liquor, drinking to my helplessness. Being unaccustomed to the poison I drowned in its misery instead. I felt foolish at my state. I could not heed to a simple request. Why did he have to be her brother?

Moinuddin was unable to explain to me the next day as to what was the outcome of my letter. Moinuddin had waited all evening to find her alone for handing over the letter. She almost snatched it from him as per his words and read it instantaneously. She needed no help to read the letter. She had a good working knowledge of the languages I had used. Moinuddin could explain to me all this but nothing of what I wanted to hear. What did I expect anyway? I really did not know.

A letter from Madhumita warmed my heart. There would be some solace I thought. We had already exchanged half a dozen letters since we parted and I was quite used to her letter form. It would also be a long one, I anticipated but too early to be in response to the last letter that I wrote about Moinuddin. I guessed all that before I tore and settled down to read. I was right; this one was dated much earlier. The letter was very long, it must have been written over a few days. She wrote about us since the time we barely knew each other. Little things that I hardly remembered. It was real fun reading all that, I was juxtaposed into her world that I had almost forgotten during the last two days. The letter continued over days and months of our relationship, till it came to something that I had not anticipated. 'We are two people so similar in our traits and so unromantic in our behavior. You for one have never looked into my insipid eyes and made them look like the most beautiful eyes in the world.'

I did not know if she was stating a fact or complaining. Yes it was indeed a fact, but then that is the way things are with different people. Romance has many dialects.

I had begun to understand woman. I would continue understanding them my whole life; I had begun to realize this too. I kept her letter in my diary, with a mixed feeling. The warmth that I had felt at receiving it was no longer discernible.

I had to get out from the state I had put myself in. I got back to my work; just a day of inaction had put my men in a state of uneasiness. There were intelligence reports of infiltrators moving all along the line of control looking for viable routes. The regular Army of the neighbor was always in denial of the fact, however they often provided covering fire to assist their infiltration. Mostly the groups were in small numbers and such was the length of the porous borders that these attempts were really difficult to plug. We had to be up to it all the time. I prepared for the nights operations in earnest. We had gained enough experience in the area, the terrain was familiar and the drills all tied up. Only complacency had to be guarded against.

"Has the rehearsal been carried out?" I enquired from Rai, a little before we had to kick off for the ambush site.

"Everyone knows his role very well sir." He gave me a confident reply.

"That's not what I asked." I was furious from within but I did not let it show its intensity, my statement was enough to convey my displeasure. I ordered a rehearsal straightaway altering the time out for operations accordingly.

The rehearsal revealed two things, one was of course the fact that many had not catered for the extra pair of warm socks that would be needed to keep them alive in this biting cold and the second most unusual thing was that I was not a part of the operation.

"You are going to lead us today?" It was a surprise expressed by all my men.

"That's what I had said in the morning." I thought I had expressed my intention in the morning itself. But they thought I was still drunk from the previous night and was making a casual remark. As an Independent Company Commander of a post, I was ordinarily not supposed to go out on routine ambushes. After the initial period of settling down, where it was essential for me to ensure that each man was up to the task I had generally followed the rule.

The situation had changed. However no one knew that it had changed. I was not sure how to brief my men. My mind was all the time wondering about the intentions of my heart. I could understand the predicament of Arjun, the great Pandav archer on the battle field of Kurukshetra. To kill a brother was not easy. He was not my brother! But he could have easily been. To shoot at an unidentified stranger who was enemy of the state, was one thing. To shoot at a fifteen year old, yes he was only fifteen when he was made to be what he was, is another thing. And he was also a brother of someone who blindly put her belief in me to the extent, that she gave away his intentions and made him venerable. I was failing in my Dharma. I walked at the head of the ambush party. Was my heart leading us to a death trap? Would my heart hesitate to pull the trigger at the crucial hour? The hesitation would cost me my life and that of my men. The fear of killing a brother could kill us all.

We reached the ambush site and waited for our prey. A week had passed after the first snow fall of the season. Two days of bright sun shine had melted the snow from around the village but large patches of snow were still remnant in the forest covered areas and on the banks of the streams. Our ambush site was located just in the centre of such an area, surrounded by chunks of ice. Selecting a good ambush site was a big challenge. In the area of responsibility there could be more than one likely route of infiltration. Which route will the infiltrator take was a matter of wild guessing. Well not exactly! The challenge was to keep the guess work to the minimum and apply military logic to the maximum extent possible. An in depth study of the area would reduce the options of the infiltrator to just a couple of routes or so. Analyzing his intention and objective would make the route more apparent. Authentic intelligence of course had no substitute. Once the route was clear, the next thing was to decide how much forward or in depth should the ambush be laid. Too close to the border has its advantages and disadvantages. The entry point would be close to his base and identifiable easily and you are unlikely to miss him. He would be coming from his safe area so would be a little complacent and not expecting you so early. However he would be able to back off easily in case of adversity for him. You may also come under his mortar fire range, which he is likely to use if the secrecy is lost.

If the ambush is too much in the rear, good surveillance systems may allow you time to readjust and channelize him into your killing zone. But if he manages to break your ambush or surprise you, he is already inside your area and a threat to you. Your ambush would be a failure as he has already achieved his aim of infiltration. It is another matter that you may be able to track and neutralize him soon. Maintaining a balance was the challenge.

A balance we had tried to attain. The night was very cold. As per the rule a local always lead an infiltrating column. Firstly he knew the ground well and secondly he was the most dispensable. Faisal was a local.

At a long distance from us the jungle indicated some very faint signs of infringement. Had they finally arrived? It could also be an unwelcome wild animal. The indicators petered away after a while.

The next night was even colder. As the cold increased so did our vigil. I came out every night and waited. I waited to find out what I would do? Would I be a tyrant in the eyes of Rashida or for my men and my duty?

Ambush was a trial of patience. I also had a battle on my mind to contend with. Has Rashida succeeded? Was Faisal on the other side posing a challenge to me? And above all, what I would do when confronted with a situation?

It happened on the night I was almost not there. The CO had called for an operational conference and I had to fall back to the base camp. A replacement had also arrived and I was almost half way out when the news of the cancellation came. I turned back to catch the ambush party as they were leaving the camp. This was my fifth night on the trot and it had begun to take its toll on me. My sixth sense told me that I had not returned without a reason. The waiting game began. Every day we changed our site; there was a possibility of being booby trapped otherwise. The site that we had chosen today was right in the middle of the jungle. The long distance indicators started coming just after mid night. There were some tell tale signs the other side of the ridge, but we could be wrong as our minds were full of anticipation and imagination. They were however enough to keep us warm and keyed up.

The infiltrator has a huge advantage of selecting his own route and time, out of the multiple options that he has. The ambush party on the other hand has to conform to the infiltrator's choice. However the advantage shifts to the man waiting, if he has got the ground right. This time we seemed to have got it right. However well trained the infiltrator may be, he gives enough time to the ambush party to prepare for the kill. We now had his foot prints clearly on our ear drums. The jungle is an ideal ground both for the trap as well as the escape. He wins who can use it better. The profile of Faisal suddenly flashed across my mind followed by that of Rashida. I lost the grip on my AK 47 for a second. The footsteps were now very obvious but they had to be picked up from the hum of the jungle. It was to their credit, there was no other sound that one normally hears from an advancing column. How so ever well prepared you may be the jungle can still surprise you. The footsteps that were reaching you were definitely the heaviest but may not be the closest to you. Out of nowhere could a man appear in front of you from behind a bush. That is the time to hold your fire, a trigger happy man may ruin all your planning and efforts.

A man appeared just hundred yards ahead of my first rifle man, Jamwal. We all saw him almost at the same time and our hearts came to our mouth. 'So close' we said to ourselves. He was well within Jamwal's firing range. Could be Faisal! I only hoped he wouldn't shoot in panic. What was going on in my mind to wish for my man not to fire? Hundred yards was not a safe bet to open fire, this was not classification firing. At night, in minus two degrees temperature, in the thick of jungle, to open fire on the first infiltrator was not professional training. My military training had taken over all my instincts and I was ready to lead the fire assault on the unsuspecting terrorists. We all waited infinitely before the second one came in our vision.

I could not allow them to come too close lest they blew themselves up right in our faces. It was getting uncomfortable and the others were nowhere to be seen. It was most unlikely that they were just the two of them. I had to take a decision. I lit up the area with flares, as the two terrorist went for cover we gunned them down. We saw the second group, but they were far too much in the rear to come under our effective fire. For some unknown reason they had stopped way far behind. That saved them and allowed them to retreat in the cover of darkness. We chased them for some distance but they soon crossed over to the safety of their side. In the process I hurt myself. The manner in which I sustained it was rather foolish and not worthy of description. However it became a topic of great discussion amongst those who did not witness it firsthand. I immediately ordered search of the two dead men. One was an Afghan, the other an elderly Kashmiri who was later identified as Sajjid from the neighbouring village. I heaved a sigh of relief. It was now that Rashida's letter began to reverberate in my thoughts. I thanked Krishna for helping mortals like us in times of adversity. If one of them was Faisal, what could I say to her? But it was not him and there was still hope. Faisal was not dead. My abject heart added 'not yet'. I limped back with victory to my credit and congratulations from one and all. The bodies were handed over to the police along with the recovered arms.

I was confined to the bed almost for two days. This was the worst period of my time in Bidar. All that I could think was my inability to find a solution to Rashida's agony.

I began drinking again. There was a sense of gloom all around me. I did not see her and she did not see me.

In these two days I received two letters. The first one was from Madhumita.

Her last letter was fresh in my mind and my unwritten reply was ringing in my ears, 'Romance has many dialects, only if one has the comprehension to understand'. I opened the letter with the notion of her having found someone, who could look into her insipid eyes and make them look the most beautiful in the world. I however was eager to know how she would convey her sentiments to me.

It was a very lengthy letter. It was indeed a welcome contribution to my state of inactivity and depression. Even longer than the one she had penned the last time. It did not speak of us and the little things that we did or did not do. It spoke of life, philosophy, birth and rebirth and what we are and what we are not. Not a single word in the seventeen page letter did she say anything about her wish to part and get along with her life. Yet every word spoke of her desire. I was thankful for not being admonished straightaway. Somewhere we had read the script of our life wrongly. Was it possible to redraft it? I was saddened by the thought of losing the joy of our friendship. Sadder than I thought I would be on receiving the news.

She concluded with her response to my last letter. 'I always knew, you were an unusual man, full of compassion and humanity. I can never match you. I would pray to god to give me a golden heart as yours. Till then I would continue to envy you'.

I knew this would happen sooner or later. It was coming to me in bits and pieces. Surely something had happened in her life that I did not know. It was probably someone who was born to be her soul mate, as she had described in her philosophy of birth and rebirth.

Or was Moinuddin the catalyst for her taking this decision?

I would not know this all my life.

The next letter had been received through Moinuddin. The last week had been so busy for me that I had spent no time with him. Yet he was always there when I looked up to see.

"Don't you go to school?" I had enquired once or twice and he had promptly shown his note books to me with the day's lesson. It was that he hardly went to play or even his home. The last two days had been totally different. I wasn't moving out anywhere nor did Moinuddin. I was catching up with my desk work and he with his studies. Often asking me to explain a mathematical equation which he was unable to solve. I was all the time contemplating of returning to the field, even with my little disability. If Faisal was killed I wanted to be the first one to know about it. And if there was even a remotest chance of saving him it should not be allowed to go in vain. I wanted to save him even at a cost.

The letter was even more beautifully crafted than the first which I had received from her.

'Sir, even if you do not heed to my request, do not kill yourself for my brother. It pains me to be a cause of your misery. Your life is much more precious. You have given so much to us already and above all a thought to ponder that the situation is not hopeless. It is not easy now to poison the young minds and many have been saved from the ill fate that had befallen on my brother. I am certain I will find my brother'.

Moinuddin stood to one side as I read the letter. His characteristic smile on the face. I knew from his demeanor that he knew each and every word of what was written in the letter. I was overwhelmed by her gesture. I looked up at Moinuddin, first he avoided my eyes, and then he giggled like a playful child.

"Did you ask her to write this?" I enquired. He shook his head vehemently. I knew he shared a genuine relationship with her. A relationship that becomes obvious between two good people.

"How does she know so much that is happening here?" I asked inquisitively.

"She does not know what is happening here, she only asks about you."

"And you tell her everything." I was a little concerned.

"No I don't tell her what you are doing and what you are going to do. I only told her that you have changed so much in the last few days. And it is not good." He spoke so responsibly that I was dumbfounded. I had never realized that Moinuddin could possibly be a potential risk to the security of our operations. He was so intimately involved with us that anyone could have targeted him to gather information from him. Yet even without any counsel or forewarning he was fully aware of his responsibility. And he was right; I had changed so much in the last few days. Moinuddin read every wrinkle on my forehead and noticed the gloom all around me better than anyone. He knew my concerns and my dilemma.

"But you should not have told her even that." I did not say it to intimidate him, but he bowed his head in a gesture of repentance. I knew it was harsh on my part; I gently patted him and added light heartedly, "As long as you do not give out my secrets, it's all right."

His face brightened up again.

"She is very concerned about you sir", he said trying to put the whole conversation in the right perspective, and then added very softly, "As you are for her."

It was indeed something that I had not acknowledged even to myself, and coming from Moinuddin it was astonishing. I fell silent for a moment. Was I supposed to agree or disagree with his observation? Should I tell him that he was wrong? Should I begin to explain him the circumstances of my concern.

"Life is very precious; we are concerned about every life." I tried to put it as best as I could. He was only partially convinced by my words.

"I know you go out every day to save his life. She does not want you to get hurt." He was very candid about it. "And she doesn't like you getting drunk." He added very hesitatingly. I began to laugh, it was stupid of me to do that, I knew no one liked it, but could not say. Only Moinuddin could tell me that.

"You haven't told her that?" I was sure he hadn't.

"No, I haven't told her." He was smiling from cheek to cheek, "But I will." He was teasing me now. I promised to myself never to make a fool of myself again as we moved out of the room.

I looked through the thin sunshine, the gentle breeze that blew over the roof tops, collected her colourful dress, as it fluttered in symphony. Moinuddin looked at me and I looked at him. 'Look she is concerned', he was telling me, 'I know' was my reply.

"I have to go to school," he said and ran off down the road.

I looked again towards the roof to confirm if we were right or wrong. She was sparkling in the morning sun. It was a beautiful moment. She stood there like always, facing the sun and her back to me silent and still, only shifting her weight from one foot to the other. The whole roof was full of colors, vibrant colors. The music was without any sound, but the jingle of her feet, as she moved, sent vibrations through me. The strings that created the notes were tuned to perfection.

I knew she was standing there for me. Not a word was spoken, nor was it feasible, yet we were in conversation. Her every gesture spoke to me in silence. 'Don't kill yourself for me'. I closed my eyes and saw her smile. The smile spread all over the mountains and the echo sounded so much like our heart beats.

The sun shine slowly evaporated to give way to heavy black clouds hanging just over our heads. The sun was playing a game of hide and seek. The weather was changing.

One moment it would be sun shine and a moment later it would be cloudy. Winter was pushing autumn out. Very thin flakes of snow would again and again fill the sky, to melt and vanish on touching the ground. It was time to frolic and romance. The mountain peaks were beginning to lower their white skirts and smoke from chimneys was getting thicker. There were no more corns to be extracted from the stem.

She was however always there on the roof from the day of her second letter. Flirting with the wind and playing with snow. The color of her dress would fade with the falling of snow, yet the energy of her feet would make it vivid and intense. She was there for me, I would imagine.

Gradually the snow on the ground would begin to congeal, fresh snow was lovely to walk on, but I would rather float. Walking in the woods with song on my lips. Small lumps of fresh snow hanging from the oak trees would often fall and slide through my skin giving me a shiver. The quiver though was not always due to the cold. Tiny birds sat on branch tops, singing melodious songs into my ears.

As the winds became intense and blew over me to the roof top she clenched her dress with all her might and wrapped it tightly around her. I felt so close to her. When she walked on her nimble feet on the roof kicking up the snow it was an invitation to join her, braving the distance of the roof tops.

The successful ambush had caused such a flutter that it was impossible for anyone to dare take a chance against us. Yet, we were cautious; I continued heavy patrolling for area domination and at times send out ambush parties. I did not however try to kill myself as it was asked of me by her. The thought of Faisal always lingered in my mind. I was scared of such a confrontation where he would be harmed. My intelligence inputs did not give me too many details. I was not aware of what was transpiring in Faisal's world and what his plans were. The marriage of his sister was getting postponed. I was not sure for what. It could be due to the dangers posed to his life by us. I met Sher Khan to get a clearer picture of the situation. That would ease my problems. As much as I would have liked to meet him at his home, I thought it better to meet him at a common place. Such a meeting would not intimidate him. He was a gentle man humble to the core and extremely polite in his manners. He understood what I wanted from him. He was cautious in not revealing his plan or whereabouts. "He is innocent," he said, "Let him be as he is."

He was frank in accepting the threat his son faced, he however did not spell out where exactly the threat was. He did not want to offend me by naming us as the cause of his concern. What I could decipher from his conversation was that Faisal wanted to come while Sher Khan did not want him to come for the marriage.

That night had been a bad night, all hell was let loose. It thundered and snowed. We knew it was the beginning of a long drawn season. The winter had finally set in. The morning was not like morning at all, it was as dark as the night. I enquired about the safety of the people who were on duty. Thereafter I took stock of the situation around. There were partial damages to the structures but all was otherwise under control. Moinuddin did not come in the morning. It was not for him to venture out in such weather. The roof top was also vacant. The gusty weather has taken its toll, life would sparingly be seen around now, I thought. I got an idea of walking down the path to have a look and see if all was well. I had become so used to the idea of the roof top that I was naturally inclined to do that. However I discarded it straight away, it would look so obvious. I could not be so indiscreet. My poetry was only my imagination, far from reality. Just then, I saw the tiny figure of Moinuddin treading up the path. The leap and joy in his gait were missing. I knew something was amiss. He came very slowly and stood by my side. He said nothing; I waited for him to regain his breath, though he didn't seem exhausted. I was anxious to know if all was well, "What is the matter?" I asked him politely. He still didn't say anything. I looked at him intently, he was down cast.

"Why don't you say something?" I could not hold myself.

"Her brother is dead." He said, so softly but it hit me like a bolt.

"What?" I couldn't believe what he said. I looked at the roof, expecting her to come out and tell me that it was all wrong. But it did not happen, the roof remained unoccupied.

"She will not come out on the roof. She is in a state of shock." He knew I was looking for Rashida.

"This cannot be true." I was flabbergasted. "This cannot be true." I was shouting into his ears. "We haven't had an encounter since the last one." I sat down on the huge rock holding my head and intermittently looked at the roof top for an answer. How could this be true? I shouted for someone to send Rai to me immediately.

"Please find out if a terrorist by the name of Faisal has been killed somewhere?"

"I have just returned from patrolling and there is a talk of someone getting killed, but it is just a rumour. I have enquired from all the other companies and there has been no incident anywhere." Rai gave me a detailed account on the issue.

"A rumour." I repeated after him. Then I turned to inform Moinuddin, "Did you hear? It's just a rumour. No Faisal has been killed. We haven't had an encounter for miles along the border." Moinuddin was not moved. He sat with a sad stony expression on his face.

"He is dead." He announced again, firmly and finally.

"But who can kill him? Is it an accident or suicide? We have not killed him for sure." Seeing Moinuddin's steadfastness, I had to grant him something.

"They did." He said it, as if he was speaking to himself.

"They did!" I repeated, unable to believe my ears.

"Yes, they did." This time he was talking to me.

"Oh my God!" The truth struck me like a bolt again. I didn't know what to say any further. Moinuddin continued.

"He wanted to return home for ever."

"So they killed him." Moinuddin did not have to complete the story. It was so simple, and it had all begun from me. I had given this idea; they must have passed it on to Faisal. I felt responsible for his death. I was feeling guilty. Rashida would also feel the same. She had so much faith in me. She had entrusted me with the secret of her brother. I turned towards Moinuddin to ask him for all details. I wanted to know everything about Rashida. But I did not have the courage to even take her name.

"Why don't you tell me everything?" I asked him, almost pleading to tell me about her, without taking her name. Moinuddin could not tell me what I wanted to know, even if I asked him directly. How would he know what Rashida felt in her heart? How would he know how much I cared for her opinion? He was but a child.

"They are all crying!" He said and began to sob himself. For the first time I saw tears leave his eyes. I stared at the empty roof top with blank eyes.

Dark clouds had taken away all the sunshine. Somewhere right on top was the sun hidden from all of us. The snow that was beginning to fall was without any joy. It felt like the sand that was thrown to cover the coffin of the dead.

I took Moinuddin inside for shelter. The fire place was lit, but there was no warmth. We sat in silence. Our minds were filled with thoughts but words did not leave our mouth. We sat thus for a very long time. All along I repeated my desire to see her, all in my mind. I said to myself again and again, aware that such a thought was beyond imagination.

"I want to meet her." I said without logic and no conviction at all. I felt so insecure and dim-witted in front of a child.

Moinuddin wept just for a little while, he was sober and composed very soon. He tilted his head sideways and looked at me; his looks told me that he was trying to understand my request and my sincerity. What had I said? What business did I have to meet her? His questioning eyes did not allow me to repeat my request. I had hundred reasons for making that request. But I could not spell even one to myself, let alone Moinuddin. I could not repeat my request and just waited in silence.

Yes, what business did I have to meet her? Who was I? And what right did I have to interfere in anyone's life. I was living in a world of fantasy and this was real life. A roof was a protection for its inmates from sun, rain and snow; it was not a stage for romance. Rashida was a flight of my imagination which only I could recognize. That was the irony and the truth.

"She will not meet you." He said with a sigh.

"How do you know?" I questioned his confidence but without any rightful authority. He was tender and small but was not to be intimidated.

"She does not know you. How can she meet a stranger?" He said so simply. She did not know me; yes that was the real truth, I was a stranger.

"She sent me the letter of request." I was trying to prove a point to myself.

"She sent the letter to the officer for a request on grounds of sympathy." This time his voice cracked, he was not convincing enough. But he was right. I was not part of her grief. I was a stranger overlooking her house. I was in perpetual doubt about my position, unable to convince even myself, how I could persuade Moinuddin for anything.

"Are you sure, she doesn't want to meet me?" I said, almost to myself.

"Yes."

"How, do you know?" I was rather insensitive to prolong a child's agony. But I also knew a Moinuddin, who was almost an adult, sensitive and mature beyond his age. I was talking to the Moinuddin who understood me. He was melting from inside, I could see it in his eyes. They were moist and remorseful at his doggedness on being logical. They were looking at me with tenderness and honesty and telling me, 'I want her to meet you'. Very softly his lips spoke, "I just know."

We sat in the room in silence, the space all around was shouting inside us. We sat in a pool of grief that we could not share with each other convincingly. The impasse continued for a very long time. I did not have words to say what I wanted to say. And Moinuddin had said what he thought was right, in full conclusiveness. There was a huge turmoil inside both of us.

Moinuddin after a considerable time slowly got up and moved out without even looking at me. He did not say a word either. I knew he had gone back to her.

I waited for a long time with anxiety and apprehension. I was sure Moinuddin had gone to her place. He had however not indicated this to me in anyway. Was I wrong to assume things? 'Why should she come to meet a stranger?'

Many times during the wait I was certain that I was wrong. It cannot happen. Yet every time something would tell me that she would come.

What would I say to her if she did come? I had no idea.

Moinuddin came alone almost an hour later. She did not come. He was silent, dejected and downcast. I was not any way expecting her to be following Moinuddin just behind. The story on Moinuddin's face told me that it was final. She was not coming. Yet, I was inquisitive to know if there was still any hope.

"What happened?" I asked him as soon as he reached me.

He was silent, his silence spoke in pain. I stroked his head gently and ran my fingers through his ruffled hair. His eyes were full of tears, he could not speak. I could not bring myself to repeat my query. It was so evident that he had no answer.

I sat and waited, how would I know what transpired between Rashida and Moinuddin? I was lost in these thoughts when Moinuddin said something very slowly that I could not hear completely. Something I heard about her anger. I asked him to repeat what he had said.

"She is full of grief and anger." He repeated, this time a little louder.

"She is angry?" I questioned my guilt rather than his statement. She had all the right to be angry. She had lost her brother. I could understand her anger but I wanted to hear more, "She must be," I said, "is she also angry with me?" I do not know why I asked such a direct question; it was probably remorse and responsibility that I felt for the tragedy.

"She is angry with everyone, even herself." He said looking down as if that was not the only thing he wanted to say. "With me too," he added after a while.

"Even you?" I was shocked at his revelation.

"I think because I asked her to meet you." He said, rather unsure of himself. Or maybe he did not like putting the blame on me, for it was me who had asked him to do that.

I fell silent. He had pushed her too far. She was already at breaking point. I felt pity for Rashida and the little boy and annoyance at my own conduct. It was not acceptable to me. My action had been impulsive and totally devoid of logic.

"I am sorry." I could say nothing else.

"It was the first time that I have ever seen her angry. She was crying and crying all the time." Moinuddin told me. I could understand her state. It was not easy to take death of someone so young and dear easily. I felt a cloud built up in my eyes. I was feeling miserable.

"I only wanted to say sorry to her." I clarified. Moinuddin looked at me with soft eyes; there was deep sorrow in them. I put my hand on his head, he broke down.

"She pushed me out of her bed, I fell on the ground."

"She pushed you!" I was aghast, I felt wretched. I could not imagine Rashida being violent, that too with Moinuddin. She must have reached the limit of her tolerance.

I looked at Moinuddin, he stood glum faced, trying to control his sobs. I gently rubbed his cheeks trying to comfort him. My comforting only increased his sobbing. I let him cry and pour out his grief.

"I only added to her sorrow." He was saying between his sobs. I did not quite understand what he meant. "She is sad because of her brother's death, how can you add to her sorrow." I asked.

"I did! I saw it in her eyes." Moinuddin was so sure of himself. He must be right, he knew her like no one else did. She was the only person who loved her. He had said that himself. It must have hurt her to treat Moinuddin in that manner. I could see Rashida standing in misery with her fists clinched, unable to pardon herself for the unkind act. I was guilty of unpardonable excesses both towards Moinuddin and Rashida.

I stood up suddenly and came out of the room. Moinuddin became tense by my sudden action. I could feel the strain of thoughts on my face, which he could clearly read. He did not know what had upset me.

I paused to look at the roof top. The barren canvas spoke for itself. I began to walk; I had no destination in mind. Moinuddin followed me. "It was my fault," he said.

"What?" I stopped in my boots to look at him.

"It was my fault." He said it again.

"No, it is all my fault." I said with a finality that made me feel a little better. I was making a confession. I was not sure for what and why. But it somewhat relieved me of the consternation that was building up. Moinuddin's steps too became lighter. He realized that I was not angry, only sad, even more than him.

We continued to walk. Her house was not our destination. I was deliberately going the other way. We walked aimlessly. We walked without thought. We must have walked for I do not know how long. Moinuddin faithfully followed me without question or fatigue.

I do not know how, suddenly I found myself standing at the spot where once I had encountered her. I looked at Moinuddin almost accusing him of guiding me to the spot. He did not take my accusation seriously. He ran inside calling out someone's name. In a minute Sher Khan was out of the house followed by a few other men. He looked frail and cheerless. I held his shoulders and embraced his lean frame apologetically, my heart heavy with the burden of my proposition of surrender by Faisal.

He was a father who had lost his young son, but it did not show on his face. I thought he was brave. His voice was heavy as he welcomed me. I could hear the wailing of women from inside. I did not have many words to say.

"I told you my son was not a terrorist; otherwise they would not have killed him. He has given the proof of his innocence."

"What use is such a proof that takes away the life of an innocent?" I was touched by his words.

"It is better than living with a stigma of a terrorist. They killed him calling him a kafir, a traitor. I have to pardon them for their ignorance because they know not who is a Kafir. They teach hatred and Faisal stood for love. They do not know the real meaning of the sacred pronouncements."

The wailing of women had stopped. I presumed they had seen me. I was at her door steps but obviously could not enter the house. Would she come out and accept my condolence? I hoped she would but that was asking for the impossible.

Sher Khan was overwhelmed by my courtesy call. He thanked me with folded hands. I was embarrassed and unable to speak, yet it gave me satisfaction to just sit there silently and listen to the old man. By any standard I stayed for much longer than I should have. Somewhere within me, there was an optimism of being able to at least see her. But it was not to be.

The snow had been very heavy this last one week. Passes were blocked and the snowline had come down. Where once stood green pastures, blooming flowers, blue waters was all a vast expanse of whiteness. One could gaze at the expanse from a distance but not tread on. It was now next to impossible to negotiate those routes which were once so easy to walk on.

The gallons of snow made our deployment futile. We had done our task, now the nature had taken over. For the last few days we had very little to do except clear the snow from all around us to make movement possible. The village was near deserted, not many ventured out. I often stood and gazed at the barren roof tops. Was nature so unkind to me? I was sure it was not, but for that one bullet that changed everything, one roof top would not have been desolated.

The orders for our move had arrived. We began our preparations and started packing. We did not disclose our exact plans to anyone. Yet people came out to meet us. Most of them had good things to say and hoped that we would return the next year. It was not to be so; it was improbable that we would come back. I could tell them this with certainty and a smile on the face. But the idea was unnerving. I was going, never to return. I had tried everything to meet her. I knew it was impossible now, but there was no harm in making one last attempt. I sat down to write to her.

'Dear Rashida', I wrote and paused to think for a long time. Something told me that she was waiting to receive a letter from me. It was my yearning speaking to me. What else could it be?

'We are leaving in two days time. I came here on a military mission. My military training had taught me how to annihilate and defeat an enemy. I did not need much of that training here, though. What I was not taught was to find out who the real enemy was. Neither was I taught how to win over an enemy. Your brother has taught me both. Faisal has taught me that the world is the enemy of the people. The real people. And the real people must suffer to change this world. I always thought that he was our enemy. But he has won over me. Rashida, I do not know you and certainly you do not know me. We are strangers as Moinuddin told me. But I must confess I have never thought of us as strangers. From the very first day you looked so familiar. The hundred and fifty seven days that I saw you on the roof top gave me delight and heavenly bliss that is beyond description or rationale. And the twenty nine days that I did not see you, I lived on hope. Can I hope to see you one last time before I leave?'

I had written the letter with little hope. Like always she would turn down my request. Two days passed in hectic activity and diminishing hope. The day of our final departure finally arrived. The curtain of darkness had not lifted completely. Huge snowflakes were showering all around us. The village of Bidar was still in slumber, like it had once slept to welcome me.

It was long ago. Where I had stood like a conqueror, sure of myself even before the battle had begun, admiring the beauty of my Empire in the milky whiteness of the moon. Today I stood vanquished in a haze of misery, amplified by the deluge of unending snow. I did not know if I had won or lost. Would that one glimpse, if it were to happen, fulfill the desire of my heart? Or would it hurl me into further gloom. I had to bow to the moon. It was shining brightly in all its majesty sharing my despair.

I was leaving and leaving behind all that I had acquired, except that one desire. That desire would go with me today.

In all the din of my heart, stood Moinuddin, with a smile on his face. A smile that did not show any pleasure but a pain deep inside. I had to leave him behind, till I made all the arrangements for him.

I had asked his father for permission to take him along, he had broken down. His father never gained my goodwill anytime during our stay in Bidar. For that reason I met him rarely. I always blamed him for Moinuddin's woes. Seeing him cry like a child I was unsure of my feelings. I did not know why he was crying till he was able to wipe his tears and talk, "Sir I cannot believe this. You are stealing the Kohinoor of my treasury. But I am the culprit. I had already lost him to you long ago".

I felt pity for the man. The father in him acknowledged his guilt. He was miserable losing his son. I too felt guilty. "Let me live with him for a few more days, then you can take him, I know he wants to go with you." I thanked him and promised that he would be free to come back anytime if he chose to do so. We did not reveal much to Moinuddin on this arrangement as yet, on his father's request. He would make arrangements to send him up to Jammu and I would escort him from there.

Moinuddin did not know of our intentions. His tiny eyes were full of invisible tears. I saluted my son but he did not return my salute, just continued to smile. In his perception it would have been the last salute. He did not want that to happen.

My eyes would time and again move over the roof top. There was not enough light around, but enough to know that the roof top was deserted. There was hectic activity amongst my men. Everyone was lined up to move, the going would be very slow so we had to move early. The snow had put us in a quandary whether to wait or move. The decision was also in a way guided by the roof top.

There was no corn, no stem and neither anyone to separate them. And there also seemed no hope. Loaded with the burden of my melancholy the vehicles began to crawl on the slippery hill road. The non skid chains tied to the tyres making horrible music. The barren roof top bid me a reluctant farewell.

The winding roads took us a long time to negotiate. The view of Bidar would vanish and then re-emerge time and again. Rashida floated over the roofs, only in image, not in form. She danced to the tune of my heart beat, holding her flowing dress with tender fingers. I could almost hear her voice and see her delicate lips move as she sang a farewell song. I knew it was only a delusion but it kept the dream alive. Hoping that the flight of imagination may turn real.

As the last bend on the road approached, my heart sank to the depths of despair. The vision of the roof would be lost forever. I wanted the time to freeze. I blinked my eyes to pray to God and salute her and the disappearing valley of Bidar.

That one moment was a moment of infinite bliss. My heart quivered. There was something to happen. My eyes took time to notice what my heart had already seen. There stood on the roof top a form of Rashida. It was her, in flesh and blood.

She stood there not separating any corns from the stem. She stood not with her back to me. She stood there not for the snow. She stood there despite the snow. She was there just to honor my request.

She shrieked at the top of her voice to draw my attention. Her shout was so loud that I almost heard it. She did not have to tell me that she was there. There was no one who could tell me that she was there. I just knew it that she was on the roof top.

She raised her hands and waved at me.

It was the first ever time this had happened. She was in real dialogue with me, in whatever manner and from whatever distance, it was a direct communication between the two of us. Even in a desperate situation like this, the moment was enough to trigger an avalanche.

Snow from the dangerous slopes began to move. Huge chunks of snow came on top of us from nowhere. Fresh snow accumulated on the edge of the cliff could not bear its weight as my heart could not embrace the flood of excitement caused by her gesture.

The snow came and buried my jeep which was at the tail of the convoy. I was blinded and trapped. I did not care for what was to happen to me. I was worried I would lose her. She would be gone. For the second time I had looked into her eyes even though from such a distance. The first time I had lost my wits and the second time almost my life. I would not have come out so quickly from the burial for the sake of my own life. I was out of the vehicle and cover of snow, in no time for her. I looked again, the roof top was unoccupied.

She was gone.

BOOK TWO

"The army has arrived in the village." Moinuddin shouted at the top of his voice from across the road. I looked out of my window and saw him run up the hill, leaving behind a trail of excitement. The arrival of the army meant many things to me. A tinge of excitement of course; but also an overwhelming sense of betrayal. I had lost my brother amid their fight. I loved him dearly.

Where was the army when they were taking him away?

I had always thought that the army was a symbol of pride. I had wanted Faisal to join the army. An old calendar with a soldier saluting the national flag was embedded in my childhood memory. The soldier resembled my brother so much. My hope was shattered that night. They took him because he was strong and big. He would help them fight the kafirs. In the name of Allah they took him away. 'The Army was killing our brothers and sisters', insisted the terrorists. Everyone was too frightened to understand their logic or counter it. Neither did they want anyone to grasp the real truth. Honestly speaking they didn't care for anything or anyone. All they wanted was, men to join them and fight for their cause. 'We will be free one day,' they proclaimed.

I wanted to die that very night. There was no point in living like this. I cried at our helplessness. Why doesn't someone protect us? Why there was no rule of law? I cursed our police and the security forces. Where have they all gone?

Why did they not protect us? Were they as bad as everyone said they were? Were they only for themselves?

Life for us wasn't the same from that moment. Misery was part of our daily routine. Misery before misery and misery after misery! Life was suspended with a slender thread; it could snap anytime and destroy whatever was left of our lives. Time refused to move forward. Our wounds remained raw and open, bleeding all the time. It was hard to understand how people could outlive such tragedies.

'Please bring back my brother.' I would cry and tell Abba Jaan whenever the pain became unbearable. He would helplessly jerk his shoulders and look up for Allah's intervention.

Abba Jaan's helplessness could not be Allah's failing. I still had faith in him, although it had taken a beating. The Almighty however has his own ways. He is always there for you, only it is difficult to understand what he does for you. Moinuddin was Allah's gift. I did not realize how and when Moinuddin walked into my life. I did not thank Allah for his benevolence because I was ignorant, as we all are. The realization came slowly and after so much time.

I stood at the window for a long time wondering if it was right to feel that little excitement that I felt. Will the army help rescue my brother? Was it an impossible dream? I picked up the basket full of fresh maize with wild thoughts giving me a glimmer of hope. I spread the cloth that contained semi-dry corn, to allow it to dry up on the roof. Dried up corn was essential for us for the winter. There was hardly any winter crop grown in this area. I loved separating corn from its stem. It was a time consuming activity and time was what I needed to consume. The roof top opened my mind and gave me the limitless sky to converse with. The big golden corns were my dear friends, so smooth and glittering like jewels embedded in a necklace. When I rumbled the separated corns between my palms, it gave me infinite pleasure.

Will I see my brother some day? I wanted to shout at the top of my voice. Would someone listen to my request please? The gentle warmth of the morning sun was reassuring but everything else was cold.

My father was a good man; he had swallowed the pain of loss of his son without complaining to anyone. Mother co existed with Faisal's memories, like a child fed on fantasies. My sister and I suffered with a restive rage within us. I was unable to make a compromise with life. My existence was merely for the sake of living. Moinuddin was the only flower amidst the cactus of my life. "Did you see them?" I asked in the evening when he came over to meet me.

"Yes from very far, everyone is scared to go near them."

"What do they do?" I asked.

"They stand with their guns pointing at our houses." He showed me a posture that seemed offensive and threatening.

That was strange, I thought, why should they point their guns at us? Are they our enemy?

"Masood, my friend told me that they also go in the jungle." Monuddin added as an afterthought.

"What for?" I asked him.

"I don't know." He said. I wondered if they went in the jungle looking for Faisal. It was where the terrorists normally hide. I was scared. If they find him in the jungle they would surely kill him.

The next day he came and gave me more input about the army. 'The army goes from house to house at night to see what people are doing. Masood saw them when he came out of his house for the natures call. He was very scared'. The information was not at all encouraging; it did not give me any great hope. Only my fears increased for Faisal.

Moinuddin was back with more news two days later, this time his information really stunned me.

"I met the officer today." He told me. I didn't believe him, "You are making up a story." I said.

"I did meet him; he took me to his camp and gave me sweets." I did not take his words seriously. Is it possible that an army officer will take a village boy to his camp and give him sweets? "You are making it very interesting, I am enjoying your story, please continue."

"That is all; I have nothing else to add." He said. He seemed upset by my little sarcasm. He refused to deliberate on his visit any further.

Moinuddin often played child like pranks with me; I thought this was one of them. But he seemed very serious. His narration was however so short and unconvincing. I was restive and eager at the same time. I called him from his house after some time to satisfy my curiosity.

"You are not speaking the truth, isn't it?" I thought he would clarify, if it was meant to be a joke. He looked straight at me but said nothing. There was no humor in his looks. I knew exactly what he wanted to say. 'I am speaking the truth, that's it.' I could not insist any further.

"Sorry, I was perplexed." I apologized for doubting his version. "I thought you were joking."

"I was also confused after returning from camp." He admitted meekly, that was unusual of him.

"Why dear?" I wanted to know why he felt that way.

"He thought we were terrorists, I was very scared. He asked me so many questions which I did not understand." He was explaining his confusion.

"Terrorist!" I almost gave out a scream.

"He gave me sweets when he realized that we were not terrorists."

"How did he realize that you are not a terrorist?" I was quite disturbed by his revelations.

"I didn't ask him." Moinuddin replied innocently.

'Surely you didn't.' I said thoughtfully. He in his childlike way had narrated his experience. It had made me fearful and disenchanted. I was banking on a hopeless organization to help me. Whatever little faith I had was also gone.

The next morning there was more trouble. I was panic-stricken when I noticed a couple of people in conversation with Moinuddin outside his house. One of them was an army man. The army person was asking Moinuddin to accompany him. His father was not at home and mother did not come out. A confused and worried Moinuddin came running to me.

"They are asking me to come with them." He informed.

"Have they told you the reason?" I asked.

"No, probably they want to ask me more questions." He said. I was worried out of my skin. I couldn't stop them. By not going with them could make the situation difficult. Yesterday he had given him sweets, so he won't harm him, I tried to convince myself.

"I will send Abbu along with you." I told him and went looking for father. But by the time I could find father, they had already left with Moinuddin. The moment I located Abba Jaan, I told him the whole story.

"Please do something Abbu, I can't afford to lose another brother." Father heeded to my request, but very reluctantly, "They won't harm him." He was confident. I was restless, how could he be so sure. Didn't they pick him up yesterday for questioning? They can do anything if they can think that a ten year old could be a terrorist. I went up to the roof, to see if I could get a closer look at the army camp from top. I was in for further shock. A sniper sort of a man was keeping vigil on Moinuddin's house. I quickly ducked and sat down turning my back towards the gunman. My heart was thumping loudly. I was fearful they would hear my heartbeat. I saw from the corner of my eyes, the man's binoculars were fixed towards me. I was scared and angry. Who has told them that terrorist live in these houses? I did not know how to rescue Moinuddin. Abba Jaan was such a gentleman. He did not realize the seriousness of the situation. I looked again, the man was gone. I gathered courage and stood up. Carefully I began to look for the man. He could be hiding somewhere. I glanced around, there was no one. From where I stood, I could only see the top of the army area. However I could visualize some movement in the shadows. My edginess could make them suspicious. I decided to be calm. Quietly I sat down in my usual posture and scrutinized the area with the corner of my eye. Nothing happened for a very long time. I wondered if I was wasting precious time while Moinudddin was in trouble. Shouldn't I be doing something more for his safety. As I was about to get up, the man reappeared, he was less threatening this time. Rather his gestures seemed reasonably friendly. Meanwhile there was some commotion down below. I came down, just in time to see Moinuddin rush in and then out of his house.

"I am looking for father." He informed me, seeing the dazed look on my face.

He was in a hurry. I didn't have a heart to stop him. Was he in trouble? He was out of my sight even before I could frame a question. I was inquisitive and apprehensive. It was probably not as bad as I had thought. Moinuddin didn't look in any sort of trouble from the way he had spoken to me. Perhaps I was over reacting. He was back in no time with his father in tow. Both of them were excited. I normally avoided speaking to Moinuddin in presence of his father, but I yelled out at him from my window. "What is the matter?"

"I am going to work at the camp." He said breathlessly and vanished inside.

'Work at the army camp? What did that mean, I wondered?' When I told my sister Dhanak about it, she too was surprised. "What will that boy do there amongst those barbarians?"

Dhanak was two years my elder and was in love. Her indulgence in matters other than her own, were limited to very few syllables. She did not pay too much heed to her immediate surroundings and events. In our house, there were other members apart from the two of us. In addition to Abba and Ammi Jaan there was also my father's elder unmarried sister, Azmabua. We were so used to her presence that we hardly noticed her. She too contributed to her non existence whole heartedly. She is Allah's child, father would sometimes say about Azmabua to mother. The most popular member of our house was Jaggi, our pet goat. I had picked him up from the annual animal fair.

I loved to cuddle and play with it. Even my sister was very fond of Jaggi.

My father's brother who lived on the other side of the village was very warmhearted and caring. He along with his large family often visited our house. Abid was their eldest son. Rasool Gulam Khan was Abid's good friend. We came in contact with Rasool through our cousin. I knew Dhanak had a soft corner for Rasool. I did not see anything in Rasool what Dhanak saw. I came to know much later that they were meeting in private too. I did not approve of him till it became almost necessary. Secretively even mother approved of Rasool before I did. I was quite shocked when the fact was revealed by Dhanak. Father had no inkling of what was going on in the house. At times I was tempted to tell him all the secrets that we shared, joked about and giggled within the house when the elder men were out. He was such a simple man. I felt we were cheating him. Yet that was the way it was. I asked Dhanak one day. "Why do you love Rasool?"

"Because he loves me." She replied without blinking an eyelid.

"How do you know he loves you?" I expressed my doubt. The way Dhanak stared back at me, I felt uncomfortable. "Have you seen yourself in the mirror?" She asked. I was utterly embarrassed. 'What sort of a question was this?'

She continued without waiting for an answer from me, "Every young man of any standing in the village has a secret desire for you. But not my Rasool, is that not enough proof of his love?"

I stood in front of the mirror long after Dhanak had gone to the kitchen to prepare mutton biryani. Probably Rasool was coming in the evening. I looked into my eyes, what do men see in them? I imagined myself to be one of them. Those eyes would have taken my breath away, if I were one of them. I smiled. I knew why I was not allowed to go to the market alone while Dhanak was. I was beginning to admire Rasool. How would I find my own Rasool? It would be very difficult. Dhanak was lucky; it was pretty simple for her.

Moinuddin returned in the afternoon and came straight to me. He was very happy. He would not tire narrating the events of the day.

"What kind of work is this?" I raised my eyebrows at every sentence that Moinuddin spoke, sitting excitedly in front of me.

"I have told you precisely what the Major told me himself." Moinuddin said in explanation to my query. "I really don't understand everything myself."

"Be careful, it may be a cover up plan to exploit you." I had recently read a spy novel. I even told him about the scare I got in the morning. He was perplexed.

"How will they exploit me?" He asked innocently.

I was hard put to explain that to him. I really did not know myself. How could they exploit Moinuddin? I thought over it for almost the entire night.

The matter was however resolved over the next few days. There was nothing hidden in what the Major had communicated to Moinuddin. The Major had seen what we had not. He wanted to utilize his potential to the fore. He was doing what I had always wanted him to do. Education was so much the need of a child. The next time I went on top to spread corns in the sun, I was conscious of the foolishness I had done there, only a few days back. I looked towards the camp, everything was at peace. I felt a sense of belonging.

Moinuddin's visits to my place were reducing due to his school and stay in the army camp. Whenever he came it was only for a very short duration. He did not have time for long drawn conversations like before. I was beginning to miss him and his childlike discussions. However, that evening he came with a very pleasant smile on his face and announced, "I don't have to go to school tomorrow." I was happy to see his cheerful face. It was the first day off since he had joined school.

"What about the camp?" I asked, thinking it would be an off day from work too.

"I will go there of course; we have to clean the rifles tomorrow."

"How do you clean the rifles?" I asked.

"Rai will teach me, and then I will tell you." He promised.

"I don't want to learn how to clean rifles." I clarified, "it was just my inquisitiveness." I explained.

"Then let us go to see the deer herd in the morning."

"Where will we find them?" I was delighted at the offer.

"In the jungle, Masood has seen them; they come out in the morning." He told me. I liked his confidence.

"Will we have to go inside the jungle?" I was not sure if I could go there with Moinuddin.

"We can see them from far, at the edge of the jungle." He made a wild guess, which was quite evident from his level of confidence and slight stammer in his speech. I was prepared to take a chance. I had gone out a number of times with Dhanak and Abid to the fields. It was only a little further from there. Moreover it would be early morning.

"Okay, we will go." I confirmed the plan in hushed tone. I did not want anyone to know about it.

Very early in the morning, Moinuddin was near my window calling out for me. I slipped out of the house while the others slept. It was like running away from home. We sprinted down the lane and very soon were in the fields. We stopped to regain our breath, it was exciting. We looked back at our houses and began to laugh. Soon we were rolling with laughter on the early morning wet grass. Neither of us knew why.

It took us time to sober down, and then we continued towards the jungle. The fast flowing rivulet blocked our way. Moinuddin wanted to cross it bare feet, I stopped him. We walked upstream up to the bridge. The bridge was in a precarious state; we very carefully managed to cross it. A little further ahead he suddenly held my hand and stopped me. Just a few feet ahead of us, a young deer was grazing grass unmindful of our approaching steps. A twig broke under my feet, he realized that there was someone around; we ducked down behind a bush. He lifted his head to look for the cause of disturbance, not finding anyone, he continued grazing. As we lifted our gaze from the young one, not too far ahead, a full herd of deer met our eyes. It was a wonderful treat, we sat huddled together and watched in admiration. Not less than two dozen deer of all shapes and sizes were grazing in tranquility. I wanted to go further amidst them. We got up and slowly began to inch forward. The herd became alert; they lifted their head and looked for the intruders. Someone must have noticed us; slowly they began to drift towards the jungle. We walked with tender feet, gradually following them. The herd took us into the jungle. The trees and shrubs were becoming dense.

"Where do they live?" I was keen to know.

"In the jungle of course." Moinuddin was quick to answer.

"Where exactly in the jungle?"

"Let us follow them to their home and see." Moinuddin suggested. I looked at him to see if he was serious. I liked his idea.

"Should we?" I still wanted to confirm.

"No, let us go back." Moinuddin said very quietly in my ears, he had some idea how far we had ventured out. I did not want to go back; peacock and blackbucks also caught our vision. A white peacock began to dance not far from us. The sight was breathtaking. We stood and watched mesmerized. Finally we had to heed to our good senses, reluctantly though we decided to get back.

As we turned, the lovely fields with green grass presented a wonderful picture of splendor and magnificence. We had tiptoed on it earlier, not wanting to disturb the herd of deer. I was tempted to run all over the place and Moinuddin joined me with equal verve. It was wonderful in the fields. We lost count of the time; eventually we had to rush home before we were missed for too long. In our hurry and excitement we overlooked the fragility of the bridge. An arm of the old rusted bridge gave way throwing me off balance and almost into the stream below. Moinuddin swiftly held me to avoid a serious mishap.

"The army has promised to undertake the repair of this bridge." He informed me. I wasn't sure if army was required to repair bridges for us. Moinuddin told me that the army did many things for the people. I was impressed. The more I saw of the army, the more tempted I was to put forth the case of my brother. They would certainly do something to bring him back. We reached home to a rousing reception. But the outing was worth every bit of it.

The next day was overcast and cloudy; surprisingly I felt bright, charged with the energy of the previous day's rendezvous. Unexpected clouds had gathered over the northern ridge. I loved this weather. I rushed to the top. Fine droplets dissolved in cool breeze welcomed me. There was not a soul to be seen for miles. My long untied hair flew all over the roof. I touched the wetness of my face with my warm palms. My feet danced on the beats of nature. My mind was experiencing something extraordinary. I was lost in time, when through the haze and mist I saw a figure on a distant roof. It was someone I could recognize very distinctly now. I had company in this dreamy weather; a shiver ran down my spine. I do not know why. I went red in the face. I collected my flowing dress and my loose hair and ran down for cover.

The moments of such emancipation were rare. The house mostly rankled us. Most of the times, mother cried inconsolably. How could we comfort her? I could not even console myself, when I cried. Our lives were an attempt to drape our grief in a coat of artificial happiness. If he was dead, I thought to myself, would our misery be any less. The very thought almost choked me to death.

"Ammi don't cry, he will come back one day." I would tell her and weep silently.

The only thing that kept us going was the talk of Dhanak's wedding. Father was worried, he had very little money and there were no proposals for her. He would tell mother whenever she was in a receptive frame of mind, "I am anxious for Dhanak, however I have no such worries for Rashida." Mother would agree in her own meek way. We had forbidden her to talk about Rasool. It would be difficult for Abba to take a decision. We did not want him to be in a dilemma. Father was a simple man; he would do nothing that had not been done earlier. He could not imagine that his daughter could choose her man on her free will. I had great respect for Abbu. My admiration was not merely on the fact that he was my father. If that was the reason, many of my friends would have great respect for their fathers. It was not so. My respect was based on his goodness in addition to our relationship. I had realized lately that it was not very difficult for fathers to earn the respect of their children. Abba Jaan did not, as I thought, have to work overtime to earn my admiration. He just didn't have to be like Shabnam's father, or for that matter any father that I knew of. Abbu did not object to my reading habit. He in fact encouraged me to study further. He did not shout at Ammi or dictate his will without logic. He appreciated any good deed done by us. There was nothing else that we ever demanded of him. This was more than enough.

Abba Jaan did not differentiate between his son and daughters. He was a great influence on my brother. Faisal treated both his sisters with lot of respect, though he teased me a lot. Faisal often would come to me asking about the book I was reading. Sometimes he would discuss things that astonished me.

"What is Globalisation?" He asked me one day, returning from school.

"I don't know." I said. I really did not have much idea though I knew it was something new that was happening in the world.

"You really don't know?" He showed surprise. I was elder to him and quite fond of reading. It was rare that I gave him a negative answer to his queries.

"Really I don't know enough to be able to explain it to you."

"Should I tell you then?" He asked me, in a manner that looked as if he was taking my permission.

"Why not, if you know." I was also keen to know what he had picked up at school.

"Principal sir had come to our class. He was talking about importance of studying and working hard. He said we could get jobs and do business with outside world once Globalisation was complete. One student asked him, what was Globalisation? He said you may not understand it fully. But to us it would mean that we will be able to buy things made anywhere in the world in our local markets. Vice versa we will be able to sell our shawls anywhere. The world will become one. But only the best will survive. So study hard."

"I think I can understand what he meant; I have also read it somewhere. The barriers between countries will be slowly removed."

Faisal moved slowly to the small almirah kept in the corner of the room and picked up the old dusty globe. He wiped the dust with his hand and rotated the globe on its axis. Very thoughtfully he pointed towards the many countries that went round and round. "Does that mean that there will be only two colors on the globe, blue and green?"

"That is not possible; the countries will remain as they are."

"Then what will change?" Faisal asked.

"People may change." I had read somewhere, I told him, "They could become citizens of the world."

"Then there will be no conflict in the world?"

"That is unlikely, there will always be conflict because there will always be clash of interests." I tried to explain.

"What is that?"

"Why did Yusuf fight with you in the class?"

"What has that got to do with our discussion?" He asked a little puzzled.

"It is the same thing, why did he fight with you?"

"Because he wanted to sit next to the window."

"That is clash of interest, when there is one window and everyone wants to sit next to it. There are few windows in the world and everyone wants them."

Faisal was thoughtful for some time, and then he began to smile. "Why are you smiling?" I asked him.

"I am laughing because Yusuf is now my friend." He spoke cheerfully.

"Really, you didn't tell me, how did it happen?" I was keen to know.

"I went to the teacher and told him to make more windows in the class." Faisal narrated the episode with a broad smile on his face.

"So what did the teacher say?"

"He said, shut up and sit down." He began to laugh loudly, I joined him. "Yusuf too laughed with me at the joke and we became friends from that moment."

My eyes were full of tears. Faisal's laughing face revolved in front of my eyes. Globalization would change nothing much in this regard unless all men became Yusuf and Faisal.

Moinuddin had become conscious of my keen interest in the Army, may be because of my constant probing; though he did not fully understand the reason. I was careful not to mention anything about Faisal in my conversations with him. Someway it could affect Faisal's life. Moinuddin had also lately begun to come back a little early from the camp in the evening, for whatever reason I did not know. Maybe after the initial enthusiasm he had begun to miss me too. He would come and narrate the happenings of the day in the camp. I had never seen him so happy. He was regularly going to school. He would talk endlessly about the school. His smiling face would bring memories of Faisal back to me and my eyes would swell with tears.

"Why are you crying?" Moinuddin would ask me.

"I am not crying." I would say, wiping my tears. He would believe me but it was not easy for me to convince my bleeding heart.

Many a times I would get this urge to get up and walk up to the camp with Moinuddin and beg for my brother's return. At times I would begin to open my heart to him, but then would hold myself. He was only a child, what good would it be to take away his happiness for the sake of my misery.

One evening I found Moinuddin looking unusually sad. I asked him the reason of his sadness.

"He wants me to go with him." I was taken aback by his revelation. My mind began to race in all directions. It occurred to me as a pre-meditated conspiracy. He had planned it all; his largesse was bait for poor Moinuddin. All the goodness of the Major and the army vanished in a moment. I could not hide my despair. "Utter nonsense." I said. Moinuddin was alarmed by my sudden outburst of visible anger. He had not anticipated this reaction. He had never seen me like this before. When the emotions settled down and I gained some rationality, he quietly spoke up again.

"But I do want to go." He said in a low voice.

I looked at him in anguish, unsure if it was his misery or mine. His eyes were wandering and sadness written all over them.

"Then why are you so sad?" I was perplexed.

"I don't know?" It was a confession of his innocence.

I was not sure either. Was I fearful for his exploitation? Or sad for his sadness. Or depressed at the prospect of losing another brother. I slept that night with the uncertainty. Who could give me all those answers?

Like me, even Moinuddin was unable to find an answer. He wanted to go with the Major but he was not at ease with his own decision. There was something that was worrying him. The next morning, strains of the decision that he had taken were visible all over him. He was indisposed with high fever. I was worried; mother made a mixture which she said will help him. I visited him a number of times with the potion to bring down his fever. I could make out that his ailment was not just physical alone. There was something that disturbed him from within, but he did not know the reason himself.

I distinctly remember it was my fourth visit to his house that day. It was afternoon time and there was very little activity all around. His fever had not come down since morning. I had decided to change the medicine after this last try. As I was about to step out of my door with the cup of mixture, I heard some voices. One was that of

Moinuddin, the other I did not recognize. I took a step out of my front door and I was facing a stranger, just a few feet away from me. The stranger was in army uniform, tall and elegant. My unexpected intrusion brought their conversation to a sudden halt. For one fleeting moment his eyes caught mine. I almost lost the cup that I held in my hand. To my surprise, he turned abruptly and then he was gone. I was not sure if he intended to go even before my entering the scene or he had turned away because of me. Moinuddin went after him. He seemed to have recovered so considerably since my last visit that I was astonished.

He was the Major, undoubtedly! Moinuddin's God father. The silhouette at the army camp, as I knew him till now. He had come to see Moinuddin. Considerate and thoughtful of him. Even Moinuddin had responded to his visit so positively. He was running after him as though nothing was wrong with him at all.

In a sheer moment of thoughtlessness, I almost ran after them. Good sense stopped me in my tracks. I looked around for anyone who had captured this moment of insanity. Fortunately there was no one in the vicinity. It took me some time to put myself at ease. This was such an opportune time to tell him about Faisal. He would have surely stopped and heard what I had to say. But could I have said anything? I would have been dumbfounded. My nervousness had stopped my breath, I was unable to even think let alone speak. What was the reason of my anxiety? I could not be sure.

Moinuddin told me earlier that he had decided to go with the Major whenever the army left Bidar. I had been apprehensive, sad and unsure about his decision. I was not fearful or insecure anymore now. I only felt lonely. My heart told me he would let no harm come to Moinuddin. Such was the impact of the fleeting second that I looked into his eyes.

The roof top acquired a different dimension for me after that day. I spent a lot more time separating corns. I often wondered if he knew that I waited for him to make an appearance even much beyond the time I would normally spend there. He did not disappoint me any day. He was always present when I wanted him to be there. Had he seen in my eyes, what I had seen in his?

Dhanak was rather disappointed that nothing was being done by anyone to further the cause of her marriage. She was fearful that someday Abba would find a suitable match and she would not be able to refuse. I decided to take a lead. It was one such evening when the elder men folk were away from home, I found it appropriate to take the initiative. Dhanak was taken by surprise to find all our cousins and Rasool in our backyard. It was the time of Ramzan, a time to get together and pray. She thought it was a chanced meeting of the youngsters. The agenda was however more than just that, she realized very soon.

"It's time Rasool declared his willingness to marry Dhanak." Abid was unambiguous in his declaration. He was the eldest of my uncle's children, though only nineteen years old. He was the closest to Rasool. They became friends for the love of sports, even though there was six years difference in their ages. Little Nazia, Abid's very young sister always supported her brother; she too was very fond of Rasool.

"I want to wear a pink dress on their marriage." She declared, holding Jaggi playfully in her lap.

"I don't think it is so easy, I know uncle Sher Khan. He is such a simple, god fearing man. He would always take the opinion of elders. Elders may not take kindly to this alliance for some reason or the other." Ali was father's second sister's son; he was mature and worldly wise. He lived mostly in Rajouri but was here for a few days.

"Why can't we make it look like the good old traditional way? Some elder can propose Rasool's name and father will then readily agree." That was Abid's idea again. He took upon himself the whole responsibility of giving ideas.

"Which elder will propose the name of such a useless unemployed fellow like me?" Rasool said it so seriously that everyone burst out laughing. He was a very simple soul.

"Who says you are useless?" I didn't want anyone to make fun of Rasool. "You will get a job sooner or later." Rasool had obtained a college degree from Rajouri. He had worked hard for it under adverse conditions. He could not take up any inferior job, thoughtlessly.

"Yes, you are so well educated." Dhanak had her word, giving a sly glance towards Rasool, who was slightly embarrassed.

"You must do something to gain confidence of elders like Hammid uncle" said Ali; he was referring to Abid's father, who was a very prominent person in the village.

"Why don't you volunteer for work at the bridging site, Chacha Jaan is very passionate about such social causes." I suggested, the incident at the bridge was fresh in my mind. Abid's father was always in the forefront whenever it came to doing something for the society.

The suggestion found favour with Ali, as the basic idea was his. Dhanak was also fairly impressed with the proposal; together they began to dwell on it further.

"There is lot of enthusiasm for the project amongst the villagers; almost everyone wants it to be completed at the earliest. A lot of people will be there to see the bridge when it is done." Ali informed.

Mother served hot fried fish to everyone after a while; we ate and chirped like birds. I was keeping an eye at the door. Abba would first go to Chacha Jaan's house from the Mosque and then they would all come home. There was still sometime for us to continue our meeting.

Rasool volunteered to do social work after the meeting decided that it was an option that could work. We all parted on a happy note. Some beginning had been made. Dhanak was very elated. "I will find a very good husband for you." She promised.

Rasool not only joined the social cause, he got so profusely involved in the work that very soon he became a rallying point for the villagers. But Chacha Jaan had no idea about the part he was required to play in the whole episode. The meeting that day had not appointed anyone to ensure his role. That was one social cause that did not occur to him as important. He was not impressed by Rasool's histrionics. That was simply because he never ventured towards the bridge even once. Instead the contractor who was helping the army to rebuild the bridge offered him a position as a supervisor in his new project. Rasool was in a dilemma. What should he do? Take the job at hand or stay back and try to win over Dhanak's hand all over again. Rasool decided that Dhanak could wait and off he went to Poonch to work on the project.

Dhanak was fuming at Ali. What an idea that was?

I sat at my usual place, laughing at our stupidity and of course separating corns from the stem. He was there on the roof as usual. I wondered what he would say about our failed plan.

One cold afternoon, Moinuddin came almost jumping to my house. He was full of life. He looked so different. It was the clothes that he was wearing. He showed them to me proudly.

"Major got them for me."

I looked at the bright colored jersey he was wearing. It was wonderful. Moinuddin looked lovely in the attire. I hugged him and planted a kiss on his cheeks. He was embarrassed. Not used to visible show of emotions. His mother hardly showed any sensitivity towards him, even if she felt any attachment, which I was not sure. I always felt sad on this account; he was such a lovely child. His father loved him, but he had no time for him. Moinuddin wanted to spend some more time with me but he had to leave early because I had work to do. Mother was not well and Dhanak was preoccupied so I had to serve food to father for the night. Abbu sat silently as always and ate his food. He was a light eater and hardly spoke during his meals. Even otherwise he rarely spoke to me beyond the basic enquiries of wellbeing. I was taken by surprise when without any preamble, he spoke to me in his soft fatherly tone before finishing his meal, "Rashi, how is this boy Rasool?"

It goes to my credit that I did not drop the plate that I was holding in my hand. I was speechless, but that was not the only effect of the shock, even my mind went blank. It would be disrespectful if I did not answer. But what could my answer be? This question should have been addressed to mother. I was unprepared for anything else except a feeble denial, "I don't know, Abbu." The taste of mutton biryani that we had the other day came back in my mouth. Rasool had so diligently sat with the butcher to get the precise portion of the goat meat required for biryani. Getting the right pieces of mutton was a fine art he had inherited from his grandfather, so he said.

Abba Jaan finished his food without giving any indication or misgiving on the truthfulness of my answer. It was my conscience and guilt that caused me distress. Why did I not speak the truth? I questioned myself. Did I have anything to hide? Was I or anyone else doing anything wrong? I had said, what I did say, because my sub conscience told me that I was not to know who Rasool was. Father washed his hands and proceeded to his room quietly.

I sat and pondered. As I thought about the whole incident, I realized that father had not asked me a question. Nor did he expect a reply. My answer was inconsequential; he was merely making a statement. An affirmation to the fact that the idea of Rasool Gulam Khan was in his mind and it could be developed.

I jumped up in excitement at this new found discovery. I had to reveal this secret to Dhanak at the earliest. She was counting her money, "I have to go to Poonch and catch him by the neck. How dare he leave me in such a state?" She told me the moment I entered her room.

"And I will tell Abbu that you are not interested in him anymore." I said pinching her cheeks.

"What are you talking?"

"Yes this is what he is thinking." I explained my discovery to her. She lost count of her money, "Is it true?"

The next few days confirmed my view. The house buzzed with anticipation and a new found motivation. We never knew how it happened? Even father was not definite who gave the proposal of Rasool to him.

Preparations for the wedding started. Mother was very happy, she said we have so much to do and there is no time left. We promised to work overtime and finish all that was to be done.

Moinuddin came into our house one late evening. He silently called me to a side and put a small packet in my hand. I asked him, "What is this?"

"It's for you." He said, I was very curious while opening the packet. A pair of beautiful blue stone earrings shone from inside. My eyes popped out in astonishment. "Where did you get these from?"

"I bought them from Poonch." He was thrilled, as he told me about the earrings.

"You bought them, when did you go to Poonch?" I knew he had never gone out of Bidar.

"Major Sir bought them for me. I gave him the money." He was quick to add the money part.

"How much did they cost?" I asked him.

"Fifty rupees." I looked at the earrings again; they were of heavy precious stone, couldn't have cost so little. "Whose plan was it?"

"Are they not good?" Moinuddin was a little demoralized by my unnecessary inquiry. I took him in my arms, poor fellow; he could not understand the state of my heart. I was overawed by emotions.

"They are very good. I cannot understand why you bought them for me?" It was difficult for me to put my feelings in words.

"You are my only friend. You have given me so many gifts. Can I not give you one?" He asked innocently.

"Yes, you can." What could I say, Moinuddin always made me speechless.

I put the earrings on; the reflection in the mirror dazed me. So perfectly they adorned my face, as if they were made for me alone. Did he do this for me or did he do this for Moinuddin? I wondered about the Major's intent. The thought was flattering either way.

I gazed at myself in the mirror long after Moinuddin had gone home. Is the beauty of my face my friend or my enemy? I asked myself. I am a prisoner of my beauty. All my desires are chained to it. The beauty of my skin obstructs the path to my heart. Will anyone ever cross the obstacle and reach to its depths? I had never thought about this, till I wore the earrings. What was there in those earrings, to make me think so?

Things were happening on the wedding front reasonably satisfactorily. Often we sat discussing the marriage plans. When we sat in a huddle, the family missed Faisal badly. Mother would begin to cry and make all of us cry too. Will he come to attend the marriage? The news of Dhanak's marriage had reached Faisal, we were certain about this.

The appearances of Major at the place where I always saw him were lately getting restricted. He would just come for a few minutes in the morning. I had got pretty used to seeing him. Should I say I missed his lingering gaze and prolonged sessions of survey! Moinuddin was my only link and source of information, but he hardly gave me any news about the army camp and the Major these days. He only spoke of his own routine; there was barely any reference to him during the conversations. One day, finally I asked him about his sessions with the Major.

"They are very few, as he is so busy." He said.

He was very busy I knew that from the fact that I did not see him much. I do not know why I found myself deeply involved with the Major. Whenever I thought of Faisal, Major would come to my mind. Whenever I thought of Moinuddin, the face of that one second meeting would come into my vision. The roof and the corns, my favourite pass time, were not complete without him. Abid had told me that the army was keeping a very close watch on the line of control. It was his guess that they knew the plans of the terrorists.

I was terrified at the thought. Poor harmless Faisal, he was planning to come to meet Dhanak on her marriage. And what may happen as a consequence? My Faisal would perish for nothing. I wanted to convey my worries to the Major. I told father. He was terrified too. 'We cannot tell the army anything, they will hound us instead.' He expressed his fears.

I discreetly began to gauge the mood of the army camp in my interactions with Moinuddin. I would probe him for a long time. He did not say much directly. But I could infer from his replies, the atmosphere was war like, undoubtedly. They were undertaking a lot of activities. The vigil on the borders was continuous. It meant that they were looking out for infiltrating terrorists. Faisal's return would be termed as infiltration. I lost my sleep, could I do nothing for my brother. The army would harass us if they knew of Faisal's plans. Father had told me. They would catch Faisal.

I woke up at the dead of the night. My heart was pounding heavily. I looked all around for some solace. I wanted someone to support me in what I wanted to do. My gaze stopped at the mirror. Reflection in the mirror was in front of me. The blue almonds were shining prominently in the mirror. I looked at them with intent for a long time.

They were speaking to me. Jingling to create a music that was incoherent initially. Slowly it became pleasing to the ears. The army is not heartless; your brother will be safe, said the jingle. I held the pen in my shivering hand and began to write.

Moinuddin took the letter with strict instructions from me to deliver it only to the Major. The answer, if at all would not come quickly, I knew that. I waited for a reply anxiously for the whole day. Had I made a mistake? What would be the consequences of the letter? I had taken the risk merely on my instincts. No one else was privy to its contents. I had to suffer the punishment alone.

The reply came in the evening through Moinuddin. 'The army does not recognize a brother.' My heart sank. My appeal had no effect, they would kill him anyway. I had all along lived on hope that vanished in a minute. I was trembling with fear, what had I done? I could not share my misery with anyone. It was the end of the world for me.

My enthusiasm had completely drained out after reading the letter. I was disenchanted and downcast. How could I ever convey to Faisal, the idea to surrender. He would always be considered a terrorist and never a brother, by the army. The whole household was worried about Faisal's safety. Even though they did not know what I had done. If I told them the army's reply, there would be a pandemonium in the house. On the other hand, Rasool was having a tough time in his new job. It was tough to extract work from the labourers as a supervisor. The masters, on the other hand were uncompromising in demanding results. He had no time for romance and marriage. He rarely came to visit us. Dhanak had lost her fervor and gusto at the turn of events. With both her daughters dejected and miserable, mother's crying bouts had increased many folds. Nothing positive was happening around her and there was no one to cheer her. Ours had become like a haunted house. Each one of us was sulking within oneself.

The thought of going to the rooftop was also dreadful. I distanced myself from him as much as I could. I avoided any reference to the army camp in my discussions with Moinuddin. Although the time I spent with him was the only bit of cheer left in life. He was such a joy, but lately he too had become quiet and listless.

In the darkness that was getting darker by the day there appeared a silver lining. Like it always happens. News came from across the border that Faisal was planning to leave everything and return home. No one was sure of the authenticity of the news, but in the darkness that surrounded me it was a ray of hope. While fear for Faisal's safety pricked my heart, yet the thought of having him home filled me with great joy. We were fearful yet very thrilled.

'If he comes as a brother and surrenders, I promise no harm will come to him.' Major's words flashed in front of me. I got a shot in my arm. Is it possible that such a thing could happen?

Moinuddin had been quiet for all these days. My pessimism had not given me any time to even think of why he had been so morose? Was it anything beyond what we suffered? Or was he carrying the burden of his own misery? I do not know why I wanted to find out everything now. Why was Moinuddin sad? Was it realistic for Faisal to surrender? I wanted to know about those things too that were not in my realm. I wanted to know if my not going on the roof had been noticed by Major or not. I was not sure how a child would tell me that? Yet today I had woken up to my surroundings and I was eager to find answers. I waited for Moinuddin impatiently. He came in without a cheer, like he always did, these days. I gave him a welcome smile and he responded. I held his hand and the remaining traces of anxiety were soon gone. The child did not take long to warm up. I began to chat and soon he took over. He had been sad in response to our sadness, it was rather apparent; I did not have to make a guess. Frozen speech of many days was suddenly flowing in full stream. He talked continuously, without a pause.

"And how is the Major?" I interjected to ask in the most informal manner. I had shielded my inquiry in the casualness of my speech. He was waiting for me to raise this very subject. I had never seen him concentrate harder. He began his narrative with such verve and alacrity that I was left wondering at the necessity of my beating about the bush.

"He was very upset after writing that letter to you." It seemed Moinuddin was just waiting to tell me that. I was shocked to hear the very first piece of information. Why was he upset? There was no compulsion on him of any kind. He could have not written anything. I wanted to hear more. "He was sad that he could not help you." He continued, as if he had read my thoughts. "He did not leave his room the next day, only briefly came out to see you." There he was, I said to myself, he understands everything. Moinuddin paused to think, probably recollecting the events of that day. Something he was about to add, then refrained himself.

"Is he still sad?" The little pause gave me an opportunity to address my curiosity.

"I don't know, he is always on duty." I did not understand what he meant by duty. I wasn't sure if I was allowed to ask such details but I hesitantly inquired.

"What does he do on duty?" It was a preposterous question in the first place, I realized. How would Moinuddin know? But my intention was not that. I just wanted him to expand the word as he saw it. But Moinuddin had all answers, he was a keen observer.

"Sir is always on duty, day or night. His duty is to give orders and tell everyone what to do." He began his explanation, "For the last so many days he is always standing and giving orders. Many times he goes out himself to check if everyone is doing the right thing." He paused to gulp his saliva. I began to visualize the functioning of the army camp. I could hardly draw a coherent picture with my limited knowledge of things. Moinuddin broke my thoughts with a shocker. "He carries Faisal's photograph all the time."

"Why?" I was astonished by the information.

"So that no one kills him." He replied pointedly.

"How do you know all this?" My mind was unable to think, I was only reacting to the revelations that Moinuddin was unfolding.

"He has been telling that to everyone all the time." He gesticulated with his hands, almost meaning to say 'how come you don't know?'

How come I did not know something that was happening so close to me? They are trying to save my brother and I did not know. It was all for me. I was flabbergasted by the new found discovery. Moinuddin had not finished, I was unable to concentrate, my mind was still bewildered with the information revealed by him, yet he continued. I heard something about someone bleeding, "What did you say?" I shook my head to regain my focus, "Who is hurt?"

"Major sir was hurt fighting the terrorist yesterday?"

"Oh, God! You didn't tell me that?" I felt so ashamed at my ignorance.

"It is not that bad, he laughed at his injury." Moinuddin comforted me.

"How did it happen?" I was relieved that the injury was not serious but could not hold my curiosity. Moinuddin related the incident of the night when the injury occurred. I could not understand much of what he said. Neither did he know himself. He was only telling me what he overheard. One thing that I could understand was that Major wanted to ensure the identity of the terrorists before shooting them. It was risky and could have had serious consequences.

Moinuddin left me dazed. I remained in that state for a very long time after he was gone. How conceited were my thoughts and action. On a mere letter from a stranger they were ready to risk their own lives. My mind was spiraling with thoughts. I had kept myself in darkness while Moinuddin was all the time wanting me to see the light. I was desperate to save my brother and no one would help, so I thought. He was miserable and confused at my state. He was hesitant to break the cover of misery that I had wrapped around myself. The first opportunity he got, he let out his emotions. I saw the Major standing tall and handsome, soaked in blood. I let out a cry. My sleep had evaporated. I was mad at myself. I quietly came out of my room and tip toed up to the roof.

The darkness of the night engulfed me. Cold icy winds caught me by the ears. I stood in the midst of the dark cold night and looked towards the army camp. His shadow of many days filled my eyes. I looked for the form in the area where he was usually seen. His figure was unseen in the darkness of the night. I wanted to do something. I let the warm shawl slowly slip off my shoulders and fall on the roof floor. The shawl took away my protection. The cold entered all my pours. It was penance, but that was not enough. I untied the knot of the kaftan wrap with shivering fingers. My fingers ached but I did not relent till it was undone. It unhurriedly slipped down and fell in a heap around my ankles. I stepped out of the heap in sheer nylon; I felt so buoyant but my body began to turn into ice. I closed my eyes; water started pouring in a stream down my cheeks. The cold stabbed me; the pain caused by the prick enthralled me. My bare skin crackled. I was traversing through the clouds that came down to caress me. The solitude of night gave me a feeling of conquest. The whole world was mine. Tonight I was the queen. I flung the slippers out of my feet and stood bare foot on the roof. The feel of the floor entered me through my feet and went up to the spine. Slowly I lifted myself on my toes, higher and higher I went. A few inches made me so tall. I looked up, the sky was dark and without stars. I was reaching the sky. A thin streak of moon watched me from between the clouds. The moon was a fascinating partner as well as an appreciative audience. I began to dance on my toes. The moon held me in its arms and we danced all night.

When the night parted company with me I returned to my room. I was exhausted, but before I fell on the bed I picked up my pen and wrote a letter addressed to the Major. I walked up to Moinuddin's window and pushed in the letter. He was just waking up for the day.

I slept only little, my excitement would not allow me to. I got up and got ready quickly.

"Where are you going early in the morning?" Dhanak asked me as I put on a bright colored new dress.

"I am trying out dresses to see what I will wear for your marriage." I laughed and she was not so pleased. Dhanak was not too happy with the situation. Rasool had changed his priority. He had begun to like his work. That gave him an incentive to work harder. Marriage could be sermonized anytime; opportunity would not wait for him. Abbu was hopeful about Faisal's return. Marriage would be ideal once the uncertainty was over.

I went to the roof without the basket of maize. The sun was up. My heart missed a beat. Here I was only a little while ago on the roof and in what state? I looked around with peripatetic eyes. No evidence of my madness was discernible. I smiled; the shadow on the other side was visible now. I stood facing away, exactly where I was standing last night, on my toes. Only I did not dance as I had done last night. I looked up; my audience of the night wasn't there anymore. I knew I had a new viewer for sure. My feet moved in my mind, each step that I had performed last night. The winds grew stronger. They danced for me and around me. My dress fluttered viciously and gave company to the winds in their dance. 'Don't kill yourself for me,' I said.

I was there on the roof for him. Yet I did not want him to know that. What would he think of me? Somewhere inside however, I wanted him to know that I was there for him. What duality it was?

The days that followed were no different. The rooftop became my passion like never before. Each day brought the two of us closer. Yet we remained as far apart as we ever were.

One day I heard Abbu telling Ammi about having met the Major in the market. I tiptoed closer to find out what it was about. Abbu was impressed with the concern shown by the Army for the well being of the villagers, but he was not sure if he could tell them about Faisal's plan of coming for the marriage.

"The marriage will, however have to be postponed for the next season, as we are not sure what will happen regarding Faisal's return. I would like to give him more time" He concluded.

The first heavy snowfall of the season reminded us of the isolation and segregation awaiting us. Like Rasool many young men had already left for the plains to find jobs. The remaining would leave now. The women and the old would sit in their homes with the kangaris inside their pherans and hope for an occasional clear day to move around. There would be hardly anything to even gossip about. The children would either be constantly scolded or used for clearing snow from the door ways. I would continue to go on the roof. The snow would spur me and my imagination. I would always have company on the roof.

Dhanak asked me one day, "There are no more corns, what you do on the roof for so long?" I was tempted to tell her my secret, like she always told me hers. But I restrained myself, "I love the snow." She had no reason to believe that I was telling only half truth. The snow was falling regularly but not very heavily. I would let the snow fall on me and then shake it off. I would remember that night of madness and quiver with a smile.

The storm was gathering all around us for many days now. When days would begin to look like nights and light would fade from the sky, it would bring gloom. Such overcast days were difficult to pass. One such gloomy evening a heavy storm hit us. From somewhere came the dreaded news, 'Faisal has been killed.' How were we to believe? Mother fell unconscious even before we realized the meaning of the words. Abbu wanted to go and see for himself, even if he had to cross the border, "It is not possible!" he said. We were too shocked to think or cry. We were fighting to revive mother, our own grief was sidelined. Chacha Jaan joined us with his family on hearing the news. They were heartbroken.

Anrool Hakim came to treat mother. There was no doctor in the village. Tragedy of my brother became secondary to the crisis at hand. With great difficulty mother was revived. At last she opened her eyes. The first word she spoke brought us to realize the gravity of the tragedy, "My Faisal is dead." We were back to panicking over reports of Faisal's death, nothing was very clear. Father could not hold himself; he left to find whatever best he could. I told him not to venture in the jungle or cross the line of control. Abid went along with Abbu. We all joined mother in wailing and crying. Abbu returned almost at midnight. The moment he entered the house he burst out into tears. Mother this time was trying to console us. But we were inconsolable. How did this happen. Who killed him? It was not true. We kept repeating the same thing. The wailing continued till it was almost morning. Then one by one we slumped due to exhaustion and fell asleep. I woke up after some time to find mother already awake. She was making tea; I was surprised to see her composed. "I knew they would kill him," She said as I embraced her and cried.

The night had been a bad night in many ways. It had thundered and snowed. Winter had set in, the morning was not like morning, and it was as dark as the night. But not darker than the darkness in our lives. As the tragedy sank into me, it diminished my desire to live. How would I survive this catastrophe?

When the news spread amongst the villagers, people came to sympathize and pay their condolence. Father attended to them outside. Mother informed me about Moinuddin's visit; he had come when I was asleep, and his father had also come to pay his condolences. Moinuddin's step- mother came in with food for us. I had never seen her do something like that. But nothing made any sense to me, I just wanted to die.

I was in my room as good as dead when Moinuddin came and stood by me. I knew it was him even in my semi conscious state. He watched me in desperation. He had never seen me like this. I could feel his heart sinking. I was helpless. He sat down on the bed in silence. He continued to sit there for a long time; I was unaware of his presence till he held my hand and said, "Major Sir wants to see you."

I do not know what came over me at his words; I jerked his hand away and almost pushed him off the bed. He was taken totally by surprise. He lost his balance and fell to the ground. I burst into tears. Did I think that the army had killed him while he was crossing the border? I wasn't sure. My frustration, anger and pain had made me insane. I kept crying as Moinuddin slowly got up from the floor. Hurt in his eyes, he stood there for a long time. I did not have the courage to embrace him. I shivered and continued to cry. He left me in an even more miserable state than I was when he had come. I cried and sulked endlessly.

In the state of my madness and grief I could still hear Moinuddin's shrill voice call out for my father. It could not have been very long since the time he had left my room. Why was he calling Abbu? It was most unusual. Father had just seen off the last visitor and come in. It was the Major! He had come to our home, that's what Moinuddin was telling father. I knew he had come to meet me. He spoke to father for a long time, they sat in the outer room. He would never tell father why he had come. I could never go out unless I was called. We could never meet. I did not want to meet him either. In fact I did not even want to see him. I hated myself for this decision of mine, but I was helpless.

I wanted to suffer in my own misery. I had always thought of myself as mentally stronger than mother and Dhanak. But I was proving myself wrong. To mother Faisal was a son, who was suffering for the last eight years. His death was a shock. A shock no mother can recover from. Yet in a sense she felt that her son had been relieved from his misery. She derived her strength from this very belief. To me Faisal was not just a brother alone. Apart from being a brother whom I loved more than anything in the world, he was also my belief in justice. An innocent was punished. My faith in God had shattered. I was devastated by Faisal's death.

I had totally lost the will to live. When the will is lost, the body would not sustain for long. Only Moinuddin knew my real state, he was all the time by my side. He was unable to understand what to do. No one in the house realized my condition as all were burdened with their own grief. Days were passing. I was neither eating nor sleeping. I only pretended to eat. Nothing would go down my throat. I sulked and cried for hours in seclusion. I thought I was going to die. I had lost the courage to face life. Moinuddin brought father to my bed side when he realized that my state was critical. Abbu was appalled at the seriousness of my condition. I was dehydrated and losing my pulse.

"What have you done to yourself?" He scolded me even in the state that I was.

I was barely able to hear and understand what he said; I did not have the energy to talk. Father took me for medical treatment, whatever was available in the village but it was enough to save me. I survived.

Five days after the news of Faisal's tragic death had reached us, late at night someone knocked at our door. My condition had just stabilized, but I could not get up from my bed without help. I prodded Dhanak who was sleeping by my side to see who it could be. We were in a grip of fear. Abbu was woken up. Skeptically, father opened the door. There was no one. He was about to shut the door when he noticed someone slumped on the ground a little away from the door. The person moved a bit as father called to know who it was. The man slowly lifted himself and came forward. Father threw light on his face. He was a boy barely out of his teens. He was struggling to keep himself upright. Father helped him to sit down on the staircase. The boy was not able to speak. He was breathing heavily and looked exhausted. His body was burning with high fever. Father helped him in, and gave him water. Finally he was able to speak.

"Are you Faisal's father?" He asked at last. The mere name of Faisal made us jump.

"Where is he?" All of us almost pounced on him. He was silent again, regaining his breath. Then he looked up at us, anguish in his eyes, "You don't know?"

The hopes that had arisen at the pronouncement of his name were dashed to the ground. It was like losing my brother again. "Why did you have to come and tell us this?" I shouted at the top of my voice, barely able to stand. He had no answer, just sat dazed as mother and Dhanak began to cry. I had no energy to do so. Father patted the boy.

"Were you with him when it happened?"

"Yes." He said as his dazed eyes were fixed on me, searching something. "Rashida?" He called out, expectantly. It was a question to me directly. The fact that he knew my name struck me and everyone else at the same time. Father looked at my wonderstruck face with a question of his own. 'Do you know him?'

My reply would be irrelevant; he knew it could not be 'yes'. He returned to the more important subject. "What happened?"

"Faisal was our leader, dedicated to his job. He had gained the Master's unflinching confidence. We too had full faith in him and could follow him anywhere. We had undertaken many missions together. But at times we would get disenchanted by what we were doing, especially Faisal. To keep us focused and motivated the Mullah would recite the Holy Koran every Friday to us. He would tell us that our good deeds will be rewarded by the Almighty. Faisal always took keen interest in these sermons. One day the Mullah gave a copy of the Holy Koran to Faisal and said, you are the 'blessed one', from now you will read this to your friends. Like everything else Faisal took the task to heart. He would sit for a long time with the holy book. Many times he would sit with Maulviji and discuss endlessly for hours. As he read on, he changed by the day. He would not sleep, rest or take meals in his quest for knowledge and truth.

I asked the reason for this drastic change in him. He took me to a side and told me that he could see much beyond what we all thought was the truth. He was however, in a state of confusion. He said he would tell us more when he was ready and when the time was appropriate. I was convinced by his words. We waited for the day anxiously.

One day, not very long ago, he collected us all, away from the sight of our Master, and took us to the banks of Chenab river. He told us that we were not doing the right things. I asked him what he meant by it. He said that the holy book tells us what to do and what not to do. We all know what is written in it, but blessed are those who can understand why the Almighty says so. Those who can see beyond the words are the true messengers of God. He explained to us the truth with a simple example. A knife in a surgeons hand pierces a body to perform a life saving operation while in a murderers hand pierces to kill. The tool is the same but the result is dramatically reverse. It is the intention behind an act that is right or wrong. God asks us to have compassion and humility in our actions. We must be charitable and benevolent; those are essentials for a true human being. We all were going in absolutely opposite direction. He was my leader and I followed him in what he said and did. He planned to free us from this life of hell and make us follow the right path. He planned to get us back to our homes. There were five of us and all very young, Faisal was the eldest. He chose a dark night for our escape. It would be ideal to get away. We needed to cross over with arms. A militant's surrender is easily accepted if he surrenders along with his arms. Getting a weapon for all of us was the complicated part. He had arranged for a guide and weapons with great difficulty. The Master found out our intentions just a day before we had planned to escape. They would have killed us all. Faisal stood like a rock; he fought with them giving us enough time to get away. Faisal and Anwar gave up their lives for us. Anwar was like a brother to me. Three of us escaped out of the clutches of our cruel masters. We were scared about our future; the security forces had our photographs in their files. They may not believe our story. We have nothing to prove our innocence. My friends went to their villages. I have been hiding in the jungle in search of your house for the last four days. I finally located it yesterday; today I got an opportunity to meet you. I could not have gone without telling you all about Faisal." We were listening to him in rapt attention. Hoping for a miracle to happen at the end of his story. He would return Faisal to us. But it did not happen. I was dumbstruck. So much was happening with my brother and we were ignorant. Tears were flowing like a stream from my eyes, yet I was not weeping. The boy was uncomfortable; the long narrative had exhausted him. He did not have to tell anyone anymore how he knew my name. I noticed he was almost unconscious. Father guided him in and put him on the bed. Dhanak brought hot water and food. We could make out that the boy was hungry; he had not eaten proper food for many days. Abbu had to feed him with his hands. He hardly ate anything. He had many wounds on his body, we realized. Mother made a paste of fresh turmeric and applied on his wounds. The boy's name was Hyder, he was from Kishtawar. The whole night he was in great pain. I sat and watched him continuously for most of the night. He wanted to tell me something but could barely open his mouth. His condition was deteriorating. His temperature did not come down even till the morning, his body was burning. We called in the hakim. There was no alternative. He was not sure if he could do much for him. We were greatly upset by his pronouncement. There was no place we could take him. We became helpless. I prayed for his recovery. I did not see him as Hyder, he was Faisal to me. The whole household was in deep prayer. They too thought of him as their son. Azmabua sat at Hyder's bed side and rubbed his forehead with a wet cloth for hours. Faisel's sacrifice could not go waste. The whole day passed in great anxiety. The hakim visited Hyder many times; there seemed very little hope of his recovery.

Night was falling again; I sat with Azmabua as she continued to be at Hyder's bedside almost for the whole day. She looked at my sad face, then held my hand in her hand and placed it on Hyder's head. A faint smile had lit her face.

"He will be well soon." She said very softly. Hyder was still lying in an unconscious state. I put my head on her shoulders and sobbed. She gently rubbed her hand on my cheeks. Ammi came in to ask me to have food, reluctantly I had to obey. Azmabua never ate at night. After dinner father asked me to go and sleep. "If you keep awake whole night, you will again become unwell." He said. Ammi told me she would look after Hyder at night.

I could not find sleep; images of Faisal had been revived by Hyder's narration. He was so near yet so far. I did not realize when I dozed off thinking of my brother. No one came to wake me up but I found myself sitting up on my bed. There was lot of activity in the house. I thought it may be morning. Suddenly I remembered about Hyder being unwell. I rushed to the room where he was. The whole house was awake. Hyder had just opened his eyes. Azmabua still sat at his bed side. She gave me a broad smile. He tried to sit up seeing all of us around. Father told him not to get up. Dhanak brought juice for him. He could not hold the glass; I fed him with a spoon. He took a little then felt tired. I let him rest. The worst period was over;

medicines and prayers had begun to show results. No one spoke, the atmosphere was charged with emotion. One by one everyone retired to their rooms. I sat and fed him small quantities of juice and warm water. Ammi had gone and made something for him to eat. She came with a small plate and fed him with her hands. Hyder was feeling much better. As he finished his food, he took out a small piece of cloth from his pocket. The cloth was soaked in blood. Hyder extended his arms towards me and offered the cloth. I took it hesitantly. Wrapped inside was a small pencil sharpener. I looked at the sharpener, something was familiar. Then I looked at Hyder's face. "Faisal gave it to me, to give it to you, it is yours'." He said very softly. I gave out a shriek, it was mine. I burst into tears again; I put the sharpener to my lips and kissed it. It was mine. If Hyder could return me everything that was mine. "Faisal would cry holding this to his face and say that I should not have troubled my sister so much. This is my family, he would tell me."

It was the evening of that terrible night. The night when we lost Faisal. He was in a very mischievous mood, not allowing me to do my work. I told Faisal that I will write about his mischievous ways and give it to his friends. He became even more adamant. I picked up a pencil and paper and actually started writing. I realized that the pencil was broken. I started to look for my sharpener but couldn't find it. After a few minutes the matter got resolved as always and we sat down for dinner. The dinner was barely over when the terrorist came demanding for food. Abbu hid me and my sister inside under the blanket. Faisal and father served them food. They were many of them. While leaving they took Faisal with them at gun point. No one could do anything.

The same night, a part of the group had gone into Moinuddin's house, we came to know later. They had demanded food. When they were leaving there was a scuffle after an argument, someone fired and Moinuddin's mother was hit by the bullet. She died instantaneously. He was a very small baby then.

The night came back to me, choked with grief. It was a terrible night. I was still crying holding the sharpner when Dhanak came to see if all was well. She asked me about the story of the sharpener, I was unable to speak, just cried louder and louder holding my sister in my arms.

Hyder was reasonably well by the morning, but very weak. We did not allow him to go. He was fearful, "I cannot stay any longer, the army is searching for me, I am still a terrorist in their eyes, and sooner or later they will come to know that I am here." Hyder sounded very concerned. I brushed aside all his concerns with a confidence that amazed him, "No the army will not harm you if you stay with us." Abbu looked at me; I had spoken with so much conviction and authority. He too was surprised, but added, "Yes, the army will not do you any harm as long as you are with us." Father was not as forceful as I was, but he had a reason to believe what he said. The Major had met him twice; he was a very reasonable man as Abbu put it across. Did I have a reason for my conviction? I wondered.

Hyder stayed with us for another night. I dressed his wounds and looked after him. It gave me happiness. I wanted him to stay with us longer. "My sister would be waiting for me." He said. The next day Abbu accompanied him to Poonch and put him on the bus to Jammu along with an acquaintance.

Hyder left a void in our lives. The two days that he was with us, we had nothing else on our mind except his well being. He left me with the thought of that fateful night in the form of the sharpener. Faisal must have hid the sharpener in his pocket that night. It went along with him and stayed with him for eight long years. That was the only thing he had to remind him of us. It was his 'family' as he said. I could not let go of the sharpener even for a minute. It contained the life of my brother. Two days I held the sharpener in my hand and kept crying. And prayed for the safety of Hyder.

It was not as if I did not think of the roof top during this catastrophe. But I had no enthusiasm or energy in me to do anything about it. I had always associated Major with Faisal's rescue and safety. With the death of Faisal that association had no meaning. A part of me was inclined to think so. The other part said I may be wrong in my thinking. I did not know which part to believe.

I recollected the events of that terrible day when Faisal's news had reached us. Moinuddin had tried to tell me that the Major wanted to see me. I was not in my senses. I almost pushed him out of my bed. It was appalling behavior from me. Major even came to the house. How could I meet him?

I was angry with everyone. The most with the army, till Hyder told us the truth. Hyder's revelation did not lessen our pain, but it added pride to it. I was proud of him always but now he was my hero. The world would know him through Hyder and his friends. My faith in justice was revived. Faisal has united with God; those who killed him would be answerable to Him and will have to pay for their sins.

I was amazed to receive a letter from the Major. Even more startling were its contents. I had been totally engrossed in my tragedy. I did not know of the developments around. The news about their leaving was a shock. His praise for Faisal was a surprise. I did not know how much he knew. Had he found out about Hyder and his friends? For a moment my heart sank at the possibility of Hyder having been caught. But Abbu confirmed about him reaching Jammu safely. It was very unlikely that Hyder would be troubled by anyone at his home. I prayed for his safety and well being.

The letter brought me back to reality. I was cut off from my surroundings all these days. I had gone into a cocoon, where only my brother mattered. Slowly the mind began to stabilize. I was beginning to learn to live with the idea of Faisal's death. It was very difficult. There were times I would suffocate and feel that death was at hand. I would see mother suffering, her pain was unbearable for me. But mother had been very strong. I had always thought she would break, but she had shown extreme courage.

Moinuddin had been a dutiful friend all through the difficult time. He did not speak much, just stood by my side and gave me comfort in his own childlike ways. Whatever he understood of my reaction to that day's ill temper, he never brought up the reference of Major in his little conversations with me. While handing over the letter he was hesitant. I read the letter one time to see what the content was. I read it again to understand it. One hundred and fifty seven days he had watched me on the roof top. The mention of the place took me to the day that I had first noticed him there. How I had panicked. I smiled at my stupidity. I was astonished at my ability to smile. And then I remembered the day I first saw Major outside my house with Moinuddin. That day was as fresh in my mind as ever. There was an imprint of his personality. A feeling of bonding had set in. I do not know why I felt that I could believe him and trust him. I remembered the day I had acknowledged his presence on the roof, of course without telling him, after the exchange of letters and the confusion, which was cleared by Moinuddin. That was the day both of us had realized that we stood there for each other. The memory lightened the heaviness of my head. The thoughts were refreshing. I could get some sleep that night after so many days.

The morning woke me with many more thoughts. The sadness of Faisal's death still clogged my mind. But I jumped out of bed at the thought of the Major leaving Bidar. I had not realized that two days was not a very long period. May be it had already come. I looked out of the window. It was an overcast day. It could snow anytime. In such weather, the heart should leap with joy. But there was no spring in my feet. I picked the sharpener from under my pillow and kissed it. I closed my eyes and prayed for my brother. The eyes would always pour rain when I did that and I would allow them to do that unobtrusively.

The Major's letter was also under the pillow. I opened and began to read it again. I had already read it so many times. The letter seemed so different today. It was short but conveyed so many things. The first time I read it; all things did not strike me. The army was leaving Bidar was evident but its implications had not sunk in. I did not realize that the army camp would be without its occupants. The count of our roof top encounters had amused me but the reason for such committed regularity was sinking in now. Why would someone do a thing like that? I began to wonder. If I counted the days that he had watched me, it was almost the time that the army had stepped into the village. I too had been a party to it for so long. The silhouette around the army camp had been in my vision much before the time I become conscious of it. He wanted to see me for one last time. I grasped the gravity of the request. What did he want to see me for? He had wanted to see me when my brother's news reached him. Our meeting was not feasible, yet he wanted the impossible to happen. Why does one want to do the impossible?

Could I do the unachievable? Did I want to do the unfeasible? My heart was beginning to beat faster.

The whole day I stayed with the heart pounding. I was anxious and afraid. What is it that is going to happen? I did not know. But I was in a state that did not seem normal. My hands were shivering and my limbs were shaking. I was not in control. Whenever I took a step towards the roof, the shiver would increase. 'Don't go' said my mind.

My heart would try again and again. I fell exhausted on my bed at night, unsure and perplexed. What will he get if I went to the roof, what will he do if I went there?

Above all what would I do once I was on top? I shivered from head to toe.

I slept not to sleep but only to dream. Sleep was otherwise impossible to come. I was awake and dreaming to find an answer.

In the middle of the night, lightening struck with its full force. I got up restless and shaken. The world slept. I tip toed to the roof. The moon had descended on earth. There was whiteness all around. Very slowly, undetected and unhindered the snowflakes continued to fall. The snow settled on my face and turned into droplets. I was alive. The drops seeped into my skin. The chill caused by the frozen water gave me a shiver. I continued to tremble at the thought of his request to come to the roof top for one last time.

What will he do when I come on the roof in the morning? It would be his last chance. Then he would be gone. I looked at the army camp through the darkness and the snow. There was emptiness all around. An uncertainty that was nerve wrecking.

He would see me on the roof for the last time! My heart was pumping, not due to the cold alone. I repeated his letter in my mind over and over again. His face was in front of my snow filled eyes. Very soon he would be there waiting for me. What would he do?

I returned to my bed and sat on my knees and prayed. Something was to happen. I did not know what. I thought of it again and again. I could see the light, far away, very bright. The light was enlightening my soul.

God, he was in love!

I got up and looked at the mirror in the darkness. The image was clear and the eyes were bright.

I looked deep inside. The mirror that filled with my reflection was exciting and flattering. Can anyone fall in love with this portrait merely by a fleeting glance? I closed my eyes and tried to imagine. I did not get an answer. No, it must be more than just that. I took out the long stone earrings and wore them. The image in the mirror transformed. No, it was much more than just a fleeting glance, I was rather sure.

I sat on my knees again waiting for the morning to happen. The morning was unlike any other morning. It was dark and full of snow. I looked out of the window. It was terrible.

With thumping heart I got up to go. "Don't step out in this terrible weather." Warned father. I retrenched myself. Many a times I tried till finally I was able to slip out unnoticed. There was no difference outside from my last visit except that the sky had shed some darkness. The army camp was deserted. I held my breath and waited. Will he come out? I could not bear the wait. I closed my eyes and prayed. He would come out and see me, that is what he wanted. I could not keep my eyes closed for long, my heart was pounding. I opened my eyes and then I noticed the trail of army vehicles leaving the hills of Bidar.

They were gone. Yes almost gone. I had failed to fulfill his last request. I broke my heart, more than his. The vehicles were vanishing one by one around the bend. Only the last vehicle remained. I screamed and lifted my arm to wave in one last desperate attempt. Would he see me? Would he stop?

That is when the avalanche came. Avalanches rarely occur during the snowfall. Yet the snow came gushing down and engulfed the vehicle that was in my view. I almost fell from the top seeing the disaster. The vehicle had vanished from my sight. What happened to the people inside? Who was inside? He was definitely in the vehicle.

My mind was not working. What was I to do? What was I to do for someone who was in love with me? For someone, who I was in love with?

I jumped, without thought or fear, onto the snow beneath.

BOOK THREE

Major Raj Singh Rathore was treading slowly behind the long convoy of vehicles that had embarked on their return journey from Bidar. The vehicles seemed reluctant to move forward. For the past six months Bidar had been their home. His eyes were constantly fixed at the village and particularly searching for Rashida. He had lost all hope of seeing her. Who was Rashida and why did he want to see her? He had no definite answer to the question. At best he could describe her as a dream that came back to him again and again. It was her constant reoccurrence in his life, in one form or the other that made her omnipresent and a very special person. Her existence almost became synonymous to his stay in Bidar. What would Bidar have been without her? He wanted to see her for one last time. He had no right to ask for anything more than that. It was within her power to grant him this wish. But it seemed that it was not to be.

It was the last bend where it happened. He saw her. But before he could wave to her and acknowledge her presence, the avalanche came. The snow came on to him from all directions. It was a miracle that his vehicle did not go down from the road along with the snow. He did not take time to get out of the vehicle. He was covered in snow from head to toe. His driver was still struggling to pull himself out. Major Raj gave a big heave and pulled him out. "Clear the vehicle quickly." He ordered and looked in the direction where Rashida should have been.

The roof top was empty.

He began to look for her all over the place, rubbing his eyes, had he seen a mirage. His heart would not take that for an answer. It was not possible; it was not an illusion for sure.

He was certain she was there. She had raised her hand, shouted and waved at him. Where has she vanished? He was excited and anxious both at the same time. She had finally come to bid him good bye. All the uncertainties were finally laid to rest. She was not angry anymore. Was she ever angry with him? He could not afford her anger. She was not someone in the ordinary. She was the culmination of his entire stay in Bidar. He had expressed his feelings in the letter, though only indirectly. He was not sure how much had Rashida grasped from the contents of the letter. Her one glimpse had given him great warmth. But he had lost her in no time. He wanted to see her and keep seeing her till her imprint could last for a life time. She was the imprint of Bidar and all that it had to offer. But she was nowhere; he was desperately searching all over the place. Had the winds swept her away or the snow engulfed her.

He wanted to see her. Why was she hiding from him? Now that she had decided to come out, what was it that was keeping her away? The snow was coming down heavily, the vision was obscure, will he be able to see her? So many thoughts clustered his mind. Her safety was of prime concern. Did she need help? He was beginning to get worried.

Then finally he saw her; it was a great relief. She was there in flesh and blood, down in the snow field. She was running towards him. As much as the fresh snow allowed her to run. There was no route, the snow had covered everything. She was still moving, finding a way as best as could be found. He did not expect her to leave her house; was she actually coming to meet him? He was overwhelmed yet apprehensive at her act of boldness. Why did she choose to do this?

The snowflakes continued to fall. With every step, she went deeper. The snow was up to her ankles. Yet she was unrelenting. She struggled and she sank. It was a bout with the snow. Winning less and losing more.

Raj stood helplessly and watched. The distance between her house and the winding road was not very much. The snow had made it a hundred times further. Her will was however unstoppable. She was but a few hundred yards from where he stood but it was next to impossible for her to reach him. Rashida was already knee deep and barely able to move. Yet she made brave attempts to advance.

Was he required to do something? Raj's mind had blanked out, it gave him no directions. Was he supposed to tell her to go back? Or should he encourage her to come to him? Was he required to help her? He did not give any answers to himself for any of those questions, just stood like a mute spectator. The only question that came again and again to him was, 'why was she doing this?'

And suddenly she went deep into snow. It was a crater with loose snow which she could not see. Raj needed no command from his mind for action. He jumped from the road, sliding down the slope, taking the high ground to reach the spot in no time. Was he already late? He cursed himself for his inaction so far. Why did he wait for so long?

Rashida had jumped without any thought or consideration. She did not know what her next step would be. All she knew was that she had almost failed to live up to the single request of the Major. He had not asked for the moon. He had done much beyond the call of his duty to ensure that Faisal could be saved. The Major was all that men should be. He was an inspiration and much more for her. She had to fulfill his request at all cost. Rashida ran as hard she could. She would reach him, surely. The crater came in her way. The snow had covered it. She stepped on the loose snow and went down. The impact of the fall buried her completely. She was surrounded by darkness, but determined not to be defeated by misfortune. With all her strength she pulled up her face and tried to free herself from the snow. Rashida wanted to see him at all cost. She could not die so easily. With great difficulty she was able to get her face out from the snow. But that was all she was able to do. She was still deep inside, up to her waist. Her struggle to come out of the crater did not succeed.

Raj pulled out his jacket and spread it on the snow and rolled over to reach her. The fresh snow was kind on him; he did not sink in like Rashida.

Raj looked at her as she slowly opened her eyes, still half buried. She looked at him. Amazement in her eyes replacing the snow. From where had he descended? She did not fall in the ditch with him, she was certain.

He was horror-struck at her state. Her hair, her shoulders, her face were all full of snow. How did she manage to fight the crater? Where did she get the strength to come out of it? Only partially, though. He wondered.

She stared at him, wide eyed. Yes, he was the man. The distance between the two had ceased. She was in the crater with him. The closeness was momentarily embarrassing. She had never been so close to anyone. The oddness did not last long. She was not stuck in snow on her own will. There was no cause for discomfiture on the account of closeness to anyone. She closed her eyes for a second to clear her mind of any awkwardness arising out of the situation and then opened them to a fresh new world. The world she had only imagined but never thought as a reality. The world where she was the queen of her destiny.

Raj was scared for her, if she remained in that condition for some more time, her blood would clot. But he found no fear in her eyes. Her courage was insurmountable. He moved in closer to pull her out. She shook her head to clear the snow that was all over her. The snow flew all around; it even went into his eyes. She gave a concerned smile of apology. The snow in his eyes caused a quiver that went down the spine. He had never expected that she would smile at him in this adversity. Her smile was unequivocally the most delightful that he had ever seen. He wanted the smile to last forever. It was not just her smile; her face was unmistakably the most captivating too. The mystery girl whom but for a fleeting glance he had never seen. She was helplessly half buried in the snow inches away from him. He was looking into her eyes; she was looking into his. He was dazed and paralyzed. She was immobilized yet smiling. His shock turned into fascination, the attraction that had always been, came to the fore. Her smile turned into glee. He extended his arms to help her out, she offered him no assistance, just continued to smile on and on. It was his responsibility to pull her out; she was under no such obligation to be rescued. Her smile said that she could die looking into his eyes. He could not break her heart. He allowed her to do what she wished.

He barely had any other option. He was captivated to a state of immobilization himself. She wanted to die, so would he, along with her. Her eyes were large and beautiful. The eyes that could drown anyone in them even in a world where there was no force of gravity.

His mind was rescuing her from the crater while his body and soul were sinking deep into a world of fantasy, woven by her charm. She was beautiful beyond description. He was at a loss to convince himself that he had been gazing at the most beautiful woman on the earth. The girl on the roof. It was an incredible feeling. He looked at her again with the new realization. He could continue doing so all his life.

The whirling winds picked the snow and created a storm all around them. It was hazy and dark, rather dreadful. But she continued to smile.

"Are you not scared?" He asked her. She shook her head, the pleasing wide smile would not leave her face.

He looked up, the sky was full of snow, eyes could not see beyond a few feet. Not a soul was seen for miles. Who would venture out in such weather? She was not scared, it was unbelievable. But she was telling the truth. There was no fear in her eyes.

"It is so scary to be out here in such a state at this time." He wanted to compliment her for showing so much courage.

"I was scared but not anymore." At last she spoke. They were her first words; it seemed like petals falling from her delicate lips.

"You were scared." He repeated her words with a pang in his heart. The thought of her being scared brought a feeling of tenderness and anxiety. He extended his arms and held her hand gently. Ferocious winds forced them to close their eyes. Her delicate cold fingers ignited him. The world was in his grip. She clasped his hand firmly. The flow of blood doubled in his veins.

"I was afraid you would not stop for me." She said. He opened his eyes to make sure he was not dreaming.

Rashida was there in front of him, her smile intact. "I was scared I would not have the courage to come to you." She continued to express her fears. He could not believe what he heard. She knew he could not believe his ears. Even she could not believe what she said. But she had said it. She was excited and happy. He was looking at her and she loved it. Very gently she pulled her hand away from his, he reluctantly let it go. He did not like the idea of letting her hand go. She was conscious of his feelings. She broadened her smile to compensate him. Slowly she undid her scarf and pointed towards her exposed ears. The blue almond earrings shone brightly, hanging from her earlobes. His eyes popped out. He had never imagined they would look so beautiful on her. He smiled in appreciation. "Aren't they pretty?" She asked. He was speechless, fumbling for polite words, standing in the centre of a blizzard.

"They look gorgeous on you." He spoke after a while. He was not exaggerating; he reminded himself, the words were insufficient to justify her beauty. They looked exquisite. He just stood there and gazed.

"Will you not take me out of here?" Her innocent appeal brought him back to the snow storm. She said it on purpose; she had never felt like this ever. Rashida could continue to stay in the crater all her life if he stood by and watched her thus.

He took both her hands and gently began to pull her out of the crater. It was not easy but he was strong. He got her out in no time. She was unable to stand, her feet were frozen. He warmed them with his hands. She loved his indulgence. He made her stand again. She was still unable to do so or she did not want to. He lifted her in his arms. Rashida quivered. He too could feel the vibration down to his feet.

"I will take you home." He said and walked out of the crater.

"I am already at home," she said shyly, "in your wonderful arms."

That was the beginning of their romance and this is the end of the story.

Afterword

Standing on top of a small mound not very far away, watching the entire saga of this romance was Moinuddin, smiling to himself. Alongside stood his friend, guide and philosopher Masood Ansari, for once all at sea.

Moinuddin always wanted this to happen. He had been pretty restless for the last few days. The future seemed so uncertain. In his entire world he had only three friends. Masood, Rashida and Major Rathore. And one of them was leaving him forever. He was to leave with him but Major had not spoken anything about it. When Moinuddin asked him about it two days back, Major had replied, "Your father will tell you." Moinuddin did not have the courage to ask his father. He had however packed his little belongings, and waited patiently for someone to tell him what to do. He was the darling of the camp; everyone had given him a parting gift. Rai had presented him a watch and Salim had painted a portrait of Moinuddin. Hari had given him a warm pair of gloves. He loved their adulation. Major had not given anything but it did not bother him one bit. Major's silence was however, deafening for him. Moinuddin's father had come to his son's room the previous night. He had never seen his father in the state that he was. He hugged his son and started to cry.

"You will leave us very soon." He said and began to cry even more vociferously. Moinuddin did not understand why his father was crying. He had many questions to ask, but he had never done that before, nor could he do it now. Everything was hazy and unclear even till the morning. The Major had given him a parting salute but Moinuddin's hand refused to go up in response. He had slowly treaded behind his vehicle. Masood joined him on the road. It was Masood who drew his attention to Rashida jumping off the roof.

Moinuddin, for a moment did not know which side to go, he then began to run after the vehicles. He had to stop the Major. But he had gone very far. He took a short cut and climbed the mound so that he could shout for the Major to stop. The Major had already been stopped by the avalanche. He stood in amazement and watched the saga unfold. The two people he always wanted to be a part of his life had finally come together. Life had returned to his body and soul. He understood now that his father had cried at the thought of losing his son. The Major would take Moinuddin as promised. His face lit up with a smile.

His smile grew broader by the minute.

"Why are you smiling?" Masood asked him.

"Because finally they have met today."

"Didn't I always tell you that?"

"Yes, you did, only I could not hear."